SHAWN KELLY

Angels and Monsters

Age of Realms

For Daniel, Abigail, and Jacob.
May you always know that the war described in these pages is real,
and that you were never fighting it alone.

Love Dad

"For we do not wrestle against flesh and blood, but against principalities, against powers, against the rulers of the darkness of this age, against spiritual hosts of wickedness in the heavenly places."

Ephesians 6:12

Bible – New King James Version

Contents

Prologue

He remembered the light.

Not as a distant thing. As a place he had stood. As something that had once been his, completely and without question, and was no longer.

For him, time did not soften what had been lost. There was no mercy in the passing of ages, no slow fading of the wound. Three thousand years felt no different than the first moment he realized he could not go back. The pain did not dull. It simply was, the same today as it was at the beginning, as it would be tomorrow.

When he looked back, it was still there. But it was not the same. A third of his brothers were gone. The halls that had once rung with voices beyond counting now carried a silence that did not belong there. Heaven itself bore the wound of what had happened. He had not only lost his place in it. He had lost it as it was.

You cannot go home when home is not home anymore.

Below him the earth moved through its rhythms. Cities rising. Generations passing like breath in winter, there and gone. Humans stumbling through their brief and burning lives, carrying griefs they had no names for, reaching for something just beyond their fingertips without ever knowing what it was.

He knew what it was.

He had held it once.

He cannot reach humanity. That was the weight he carried. Not chains. Not darkness. Just distance. An unbridgeable, aching distance from everything on both sides of where he stood. Heaven behind him. Earth below him. And him, suspended between the two, unseen by all of it.

He had grown accustomed to being unseen.

And then she looked up.

Not through him. Not past him. At him. Her eyes found his across the veil with a certainty that stopped something deep inside his chest.

She could see him.

Introduction

A Word Before You Enter

There is a war happening right now.

Not the kind you read about in headlines, tracked by satellites, or debated in halls of politics. This war is older than time itself. It runs beneath every empire that has ever risen, beneath every civilization that has ever fallen, beneath every quiet moment you have ever mistaken for peace.

I did not write this book to convince you of anything. I wrote it because the stories we find in scripture, and in the texts that surround scripture, the ones most people never encounter, are extraordinary. They are raw, ancient, and alive in ways that centuries of tradition have managed to bury under layers of stained glass and familiarity.

I wanted to dig them back up.

The characters you are about to meet are not entirely invented. Seraphiel, Azazel, Lumiel, Ezekiel. These names carry weight in texts that predate most of what sits in your Bible. The Book of Enoch, the Dead Sea Scrolls, the ancient Hebrew sources that shaped the earliest understanding of the unseen world. I have tried to be faithful to those roots while giving the story room to breathe.

Within these pages you may find familiarity. You may find intrigue. You may find happiness, sadness, rage, or something you do not have a name for yet. Whatever finds you, follow it. Keep reading.

Come in.

Shawn

1

The Veil Between Realms

Introduction to the Realms

Earth, a blue jewel suspended against the vast indigo tapestry of the cosmos, glimmers with a delicate radiance that belies its fragility. From the height of the celestial realms, where the harmonious laughter of choir-like angels mingles with soft golden light, one can see the intricate web of life that thrives beneath. However, this wood-and-water bark, a cradle for humankind's aspirations and dreams, is a thin veneer over the cosmic abysses swirling with the colors of chaos and creation.

An ethereal wind whispers through the celestial corridors, as bright as the stars and as gentle as a lover's sigh, bringing with it subtle hints of the struggles that unfold just beyond the veil separating realms. In the dampened silence of celestial realms, it is here that the concept of the realms—each distinct yet intertwined—takes form. Unseen battles rage like storms upon the horizon, shakes of thunder echoing through dimensions. At the same time, mere mortals remain blissfully unaware of the thin membrane that separates reality from the infinite realms.

Ah, the veil. A delicate boundary, gossamer yet robust, inscribed with the sacred laws of creation. It is not merely a barrier but a testament to the complex dynamics between light and shadow, order and disorder. Seraphiel, a guardian of light, gazes down from the angelic heights, his soul draped in the luminous fabric of hope yet weighed by shadows of regret. He watches humanity, an amalgamation of beauty and frailty, wandering through their existence with a mixture of conviction and doubt.

"Each heartbeat is a prayer," he muses to himself, standing on the precipice where the luminescent realm meets the engulfing dark. From here, he witnesses the vibrancy of Earth—a diverse panorama of life coursing with passion and pain. Rivers of silver dissect verdant forests, mountains stand resolute against the sky, and cities pulse with the chaotic rhythm of humanity. But amidst this beauty lurks an ancient foreboding, as a tempest brews beyond the nascent borders of their understanding: monsters, born from the fabric of rebellion, roam in the realm of shadows.

Every age narrates tales of them—monsters that transformed from once-radiant beings of divine light, warped by their intentions, their hearts dulled by ambition and desires long since forsaken. To humans, they are legends; figures of myth that dance on the precipice of fear and awe. But beneath the skin of myth resides truth—monsters that crave their former glory, battling not just against the confines of their form, but against the ever-looming specter of redemption.

The contrast between the heavenly and the monstrous is stark. Where the angelic realms shimmer with light that banishes shadows—a symphony of harmonious voices intertwined in reverent echoes—there lie chaotic domains swirling with discord and tumult. Beings of despair harness the primal chaos of creation, manipulating darkness with as much fervor as angels wield light. Each realm embodies its essence, reflecting its inhabitants' desires, fears, and dreams.

Seraphiel, one of the esteemed seraphs, descends momentarily, allowing his feet to brush against the cusp of reality. Emotions whirl within him as he walks the thin line between existence and essence like a tempest. He recalls his own fall, the moment when loyalty fractured into the fragments of rebellion. Once a beacon of light, he finds himself caught in the throes of a storm, knowing the true weight of being an outsider in both the celestial and earthly realms.

The whispers of his past echo in his mind—a cacophony of laughter and betrayal, love and loathing. Seraphiel had once stood shoulder to shoulder with divine kin, guardians of harmony tasked with watching over humanity. Yet, the thrill of autonomy beckoned to him, fed by Azazel's silver-tongued words. "Freedom!" Azazel had declared—twisting sacred truths into seductive lies. The concept of free will, a gift once bestowed, morphed into an alluring sin, ushering forth rebellion. The melodies that once supported the harmony of the cosmos frayed at the edges, and Seraphiel, driven by longing and an insatiable desire for recognition, was swept away into disarray.

A familiar pain twinges in his heart as he stands astride the realms. "What does it mean to be an angel when the weight of past sins clouds the very purpose of your light?" The question resonates deeply within him, a haunting reminder that even celestial beings are not immune to doubt.

On Earth, civilizations rise and fall within a heartbeat. Kingdoms flourish beneath the gentle caress of a sun that shines equally on the just and the unjust. Yet beneath this veneer of tranquility lies an undercurrent shaped by unseen entities battling for the souls of humanity. Every shadow cast has its origin, and Seraphiel is painfully aware of the stakes involved in these silent skirmishes. The beings of chaos scheme, weaving webs of discontent, while the angels of light strive to shield humanity from the depths of despair. It is a ceaseless war fought not only in the ether but within the very fabric of existence, its strain palpable.

Tension envelops the celestial realms while echoes of ancient conflicts reverberate, reminiscent of fallen brothers and sisters who trail their glowing remnants across the cosmic currents. Seraphiel feels the emotions of a guardian swell within his being—soaring joy and profound sorrow intermingle, creating a bittersweet symphony reflective of his tumultuous past. He longs anew to reclaim his place in the angelic courts, yet, beneath it all, a desperate ache brews—a desire for forgiveness intertwined with fear.

The sight of Earth enchants him, yet it stirs a longing for a past irrevocably lost. He sees the defining edges of civilization and how humanity sculpts legends from encounters that cradle the threads of truth within imagination. The myths, clangorous in their irony, emerge—heroes forged in the fires of despair, angels who descend to uplift or trade salvation for destruction. Each story has roots in something deeper, a resonance faintly perceived, hinting at battles not won but waged in the spaces between realms.

Seraphiel embodies the tension of existence, a celestial being swinging between the allure of redemption and the burden of his fall. "How can they see us?" he laments. "How many more heroes shall rise from the ashes before we, too, find a way to soar again?"

The image of Liora pierces his aching heart, a mortal resident entrusting revelations of divinity and despair. Her dreams are a tapestry woven by fate, hinting at the connection between worlds—the fragility of time spent yearning. Liora, gifted with glimpses of other realms, faces the daunting task of decoding the divine threads that spin through her life. He marvels at her, this human with dreams too great for her mortal frame. Each vision she receives births a truth transcending the earthly; they illuminate the dark corners where monsters dwell, yet carry the potential for hope and healing.

In the heart of humanity, the light flickers despite the encompassing dark, each flicker a defiance of despair and destruction. As Seraphiel watches her navigate the corridors of both dream and reality, he feels the burden of guardianship pressing down anew. He longs to reach beyond the veil, to infuse her heart with light and ignite the aspirations within her soul. But the distance is heavy, and the ever-present veil reminds him of his monstrous inclinations.

"Perhaps freedom lies not in the light we chase but in the shadows we acknowledge," Seraphiel reflects. The ghosts of his past echo through the chasms of his heart, reminding him of the delicate balance that exists in the realms. Good and evil entwine. Angels and monsters share stories, and hearts shelter echoes of forgiveness or vengeance. The dance between creation and destruction continues in silent cadence, and like ever-thunderous waves wrapping around a bleached shore, the struggle endures.

As the sun dips below the horizon, casting a mosaic of light and shadow across Earth, Seraphiel recognizes that the thin veil is but a reflection of humanity's own experience. Each decision to embrace light over dark becomes an act of rebellion against despair, a story waiting to be told. And here, at this moment in time, the stakes could not be higher—an invitation culminating in the awakening of a new tapestry forged in the fires of conflict and revelation.

With his heart racing, Seraphiel whispers into the void, a prayer into the ether. "Guide them, Yahuah. Illuminate their choices, let them weave their narratives with threads of courage, for every action can tip the scales between light and shadow."

In this dimming light, the worlds teeter—a fragile intersection echoing with the promise of new beginnings, the whispers of heroes yet to rise entwined with the cautionary tales of those who have fallen. A glimmer of hope flickers within Seraphiel, illuminating the dawn of possibility, a testament of intertwined fate that beckons across the veil: "What if humanity holds the power to conquer both the chaos and the cosmos?"

As he gazes into the darkness surrounding Earth, he feels that deep within the human spirit flows a divine potential, an echo of the celestial that longs to shine through. The battle rages, yet with every heartbeat, there exists a chance—a thread connecting them all, woven in the fabric of multiple realms that exist in intricate dance.

"Will they awaken to their own divinity," Seraphiel wonders, "or will they cling to the chains of fear and doubt?" The questions he asks linger like memories, vivid in their resonance, poised to guide the unfolding story of realms intertwined. The thin veil shelters truths yet to unfold, shadows ready to embrace, and angels waiting to guide.

In this sacred moment, the celestial and the earthly converge, setting the stage for the epic tale yet to be told—an adventure woven through the luminance of hope, stitched together by the threads of existence, in a wondrous universe filled with trepidation. The vast expanse of the cosmos awaits, longing to witness how the entwined fates of angels and humanity shall unfold across the luminous dance of creation, held together by an ever-fragile veil.

The Nature of Angels and Monsters

The celestial hierarchy, an intricate web of power and responsibility, had once functioned seamlessly within the realms of light. At the pinnacle stood the seraphs, radiant beings of pure love and devotion, encircled by the luminescent flames of their divine essence. Each seraph was entrusted with a unique aspect of Yahuah's creation: love, wisdom, justice, and mercy. They were the guardians of divine order, weaving threads of harmony that linked all realms. Yet, amidst this ordered paradise existed the seeds of discord.

As Lumiel, the seraph of enlightenment, walked the sapphire skies of the angelic realm, he could sense the unsettling tension that permeated the air. Even as the sun of purity shone brightly, shadows danced at the edges, dark whispers spreading among the angels' wings. Among the most compelling figures was Azazel, once a mighty seraph whose charisma captivated many. His once-gleaming wings had become tainted with ambition and a hunger for autonomy that threatened the very fabric of angelic unity.

Flashbacks to a time of camaraderie flooded Lumiel's mind. He recalled the night when angels gathered to discuss the creation of humanity. They had marveled at the complexity of these beings, crafted in Yahuah's image. Each angel had contributed their gifts, infusing life into humanity with attributes of kindness, bravery, and resilience. Only Azazel remained aloof during the meeting, his mind swirling with thoughts that diverged from their collective purpose. In those moments of solitude, Azazel first entertained notions that would lead to his downfall.

"I do not understand why we are to serve these fragile creatures," Azazel had said, his voice a silken thread woven through the congregation. "We are the bearers of divine will, yet we are expected to be their mere guardians. Is it not an indignity to be subservient to beings crafted from dust?"

Lumiel had felt an icy grip around his heart at Azazel's words. They echoed with a truth that many sought to dismiss. "We are protectors by divine design. To guide humanity is our purpose, our privilege," Lumiel had countered, his resolve firm. Yet, Azazel's charm had begun to sway others even then.

The growing fissure between loyalty to Yahuah and the burgeoning idea of personal autonomy echoed across the heavenly realm. As Lumiel and his brethren watched the once-unified front fracture, they struggled with their own perceptions of what it meant to be an angel. Were they merely instruments of Yahuah's will, or did the spark of individual intention grant them rights to define their existence?

The dialogues within the celestial realm only intensified. Throughout the archways of the angelic domain, whispers filled the air, spreading Azazel's discontent like wildfire. "Are we not more than this?" he would challenge, his voice seductive and cool. "What divine being ought to be constrained by rules that do not benefit their own desires? Join me, and we can ascend far beyond our designed purposes—reshape the cosmos on our own terms."

His words coaxed others into his deceitful embrace, breathing life into a rebellion that cast long shadows upon the realm. Seraphs began to question their roles, uncertain of whom to trust. Lumiel witnessed these doubts manifest in his fellow angels, leaving them vulnerable to Azazel's enticing promises.

The seraph Ezekiel, previously a stalwart defender of divine law, found himself tormented by the turbulence of his brethren. "I cannot bear witness to our fracturing," he confessed during a gathering of the loyal seraphs, his wings drooping under the weight of despair. "All our purpose has revolved around guidance and protection—yet what is left when guidance transforms into tyranny?"

"The struggle is to find a balance," Lumiel argued, his gaze firm and unwavering. "Our role as protectors does not strip us of agency or purpose. We can influence humanity while maintaining allegiance to Yahuah."

And yet, with each passing day, the splintering faction of Azazel grew increasingly bold. The charismatic seraph was no longer one voice among many; he had amassed a following of fallen angels, those who hungered for a taste of freedom they had never known. "You see," he began during a pivotal night of deliberation, "the universe is our playground. Why sacrifice it for beings that may never comprehend our gifts? With their flawed hearts, they only bind us to their wishes, paradoxically rendering us powerless."

Through his shrewd manipulation, Azazel stoked the fires of rebellion until the moment of eruption culminated. As the celestial skies darkened, the seraphs were caught in an overwhelming torrent of conflict birthed from whispers and insidious charm.

The rebellion that followed was not merely an act against Yahuah's order but a sweeping transformation of beings once devoted to light into entities steeped in chaos and darkness. The fall was beautiful and tragic, painted in crimson and midnight blue hues, each fallen angel leaving behind a shimmering light that flickered with the memories of what they had abandoned.

While intoxicating in its enormity, Azazel's ambition was not without consequence. Through betrayal and manipulation, he coaxed his followers to turn against their brethren, promising power, freedom, and a reshaping of their identities. The battlefield became a place of visceral beauty: radiant wings splintering like glass, celestial harmonies twisted into agonizing wails. The fall that once signified greatness became synonymous with despair. They had embraced new identities—monsters born from angels' desires run awry.

In stark contrast to Azazel's chaos, Lumiel remained a beacon, his heart swollen with both grief and resolve. He struggled against the tides of rebellion, desperately trying to understand if redemption was ever possible for the beings that had once resided in divine light. Azazel, in his newfound cunning, had redefined what it meant to exist beyond the gaze of Yahuah.

Ezekiel, witnessing this unfolding tragedy, felt pulled. As a guardian angel now tasked with looking after humanity, he often found himself torn between his duties and his longing to save his conflicted brethren, especially Lumiel.

"You must understand, Ezekiel, we cannot forsake the light," Lumiel implored during a clandestine meeting. They were surrounded by remnants of the celestial order—those frail flickers of hope that struggled against overwhelming darkness. "What is lost can be reclaimed if we remain steadfast. We must stand firm against Azazel's vision of chaos."

"Azazel's allure runs deeper than any of us realized," Ezekiel replied, his voice low and heavy with foreboding. "He speaks to the hearts of angels, unearthing desires long buried. Our strength is waning, Lumiel. Perhaps rebellion is not simply a wicked impulse but an awakening to desires we have never acknowledged. What is our true purpose?"

As they debated the essence of their existence, the dichotomy between angels and monsters became starkly apparent. The faithful seraphs upheld divine law, believing in the eternal duty to shepherd humanity, a responsibility born from love—meanwhile, the fallen embraced chaos, seeking empowerment by rejecting anything binding or constricting.

The understanding of angels and monsters remained tragically skewed in the human realm. Tales spun through generations conflated the two entities. A misunderstanding seemed to envelop both supernatural beings and humanity. Once angels turned renegade, monsters wandered the earth, lurking within shadows, haunted by their choices. Humans painted their stories with brushstrokes of fear, often depicting them as villainous beings, driven solely by wickedness. But the truth lay veiled beneath layers of misconceptions—their experiences shaped by internal conflict, loss, and longing.

Ezekiel emerged as the embodiment of this struggle within the human realm. As a guardian angel, he felt their turbulent emotions seep into his existence. "You, dear humans, dwell in the world we shaped out of light, yet you remain ignorant of the darkness lurking just beyond your perceptions," he whispered, cradling a distant cry of despair. He guided those who sought him, nurturing a connection to the divine even as shadows threatened to consume the fragile line between realms.

"Do you fear what you cannot see?" he often asked the dreamers who sought guidance during moments of darkness. The fear of monsters gripped them tightly, but Ezekiel sought to unveil deeper truths. "Look beyond flesh and shadow. Not all who wear the guise of darkness are devoid of light."

Ezekiel understood that humans might fear the beings that walked alongside them—the fallen angels—and the very essence of their misconceptions often exacerbated the conflict. The mythology surrounding angels and monsters surged with falsehoods, misrepresenting their truths and underestimating their emotional struggles. Humans saw monsters as malevolent forces, utterly unaware that these beings grappled with regret, a relentless yearning for redemption mixed with fear of their own capacity for destruction.

Amidst these interwoven narratives, the truth remained that angels and monsters shared a common origin, their fates interlocked through choices made and ideologies pursued. Both were entities forged in an eternal struggle of light and darkness, yet society's perception had twisted their realities into something far more sinister.

As Lumiel reflected upon the truth of their existence, he ruminated on the words of Ezekiel: "Our identities are not defined by the realms we inhabit, but by the choices we make within them." This truth was shared with fallen angels like Azazel, who exuded an unmistakable charm even as he toyed with deception—a monster in pursuit of power yet exposed to hidden vulnerability.

In their shared experiences, the seraphs and fallen angels faced an intertwined destiny. Even as Lumiel faced the depths of loss, he strove to maintain hope, believing redemption to be the ultimate prize for even the most damned. Echoes of futures lost whispered through the winds of the celestial realm, and within every encounter, every heartache, lay the potential for growth, understanding, and the revelation of what it truly meant to be an angel—the eternal quest for light amidst darkness.

As Lumiel and Ezekiel continued their deliberations, mourning their fallen brethren, they knew a decision loomed on the horizon—one that would ripple across realms and determine the ever-blurring lines between angels and monsters. It would be a choice that could reclaim the glory of their origins or plunge them deeper into chaos. After all, in the dance of existence, the thin veil separating the realms of angels and monsters was less sturdy than anyone could imagine, anchored by their choices.

The Impact on Humanity

The sun dipped below the horizon, casting long shadows that danced across the weathered stones of an ancient village, a place steeped in myth and memory. As twilight wrapped her arms around the land, Liora felt a familiar stirring deep within her soul. It was an electric sensation, a whisper from a realm beyond her comprehension, compelling her to seek out the truths hidden in the fabric of her reality. Each day, the veil between the realms grew thinner, and the echoes of divine presence became more pronounced, blurring the lines between the mundane and the extraordinary.

The stories told by the fire on cold winter nights had always captivated her. They spoke of mighty and radiant angels who descended from the heavens, guiding humanity through the darkness. Yet, woven into these tales were the threads of caution—stories of fallen angels, their wings marred by the stains of betrayal and longing. As she listened to her elders recount these legends, Liora often pondered the duality of their existence, the intoxicating allure of heavenly grace alongside the chilling reality of their fall. Each account reflected a human tendency to search for meaning, find solace in celestial beings, and question the moral fabric of their lives.

She was not like the others in her village, trapped within the constraints of ordinary beliefs. Liora was different—gifted, yet burdened by visions that often came unbidden and without warning. Each vision felt like a thread pulled from the tapestry of time, intertwining her fate with celestial dynamics far beyond her control. On nights when the stars twinkled like diamonds against the velvet sky, she would slip away from her home, seeking solitude in the forest. There, beneath an ancient oak, she would close her eyes and surrender herself to the whispers of the divine.

This night was no different as Liora settled against the tree's gnarled trunk, the cool earth cradling her as she sought to remember the last vision that had shaken her. She had seen a great conflict unfolding, a struggle not only between celestial entities but also among the human spirit. Dark clouds loomed, threatening to engulf the sun's warmth, while a multitude of shadowy figures clashed against the brilliant light emanating from valiant angelic beings. But one figure caught her breath—a lone angel, wings tattered yet fierce, standing against the tide of chaos.

Liora feared for what she had witnessed. The dimensions were colliding, and humanity was caught in the midst of a cosmic war. But even within the frenetic turmoil of her visions, there were glimmers of hope, threads of potential woven through the fear. Perhaps she could be a beacon against the darkness—a reminder to her people of their own connection to the celestial realms. But how could she convey such truth to those who were content with their ignorance? How could she explain the weight of divine influence on their everyday lives?

She remembered the myths and stories that had shaped her understanding of the world. Elder villagers often spoke of Icarus, who flew too close to the sun, and the tragic tale of Phaethon, whose reckless driving of the sun's chariot caused chaos on Earth. Each story contained poignant truths—a commentary on humanity's ceaseless quest for knowledge and the dangers associated with reaching beyond what was deemed safe. They were warnings wrapped in lessons, each tale echoing the sentiment that while celestial beings could inspire great progress, they could also lead to dire consequences.

The presence of angels and demons has influenced humanity throughout history. From the founding of civilizations to revolutions that shook the earth, their fingerprints adorned the annals of myth and legend. Each act of divine intervention or malevolent scheme carved a new narrative in the hearts of humanity. The tradespeople of ancient cities associated their fortunes with blessings from patron saints, while warriors charged into battle with fervent prayers, hoping for divine favor. The allure of these beings defined cultures, inspired art, and ignited wars—all manifestations of humanity's desperate desire for guidance in a chaotic world.

Liora brushed her fingers against the tree bark, grounding herself in the present. Her thoughts shifted to the recent whispers she had encountered within her visions. The angel she had seen was not merely a spectator. She felt the weight of his struggles and the conflicting emotions that pulsed through him. Like the ancient tales she cherished, he embodied the complexity of light and shadow, the precarious balance of free will and divine purpose. Through him, Liora realized that her journey mirrored the struggles both angels and humans face—a desire for understanding intertwined with the fear of consequence.

For too long, she had remained an observer in her own life, a passive participant. But the urgency of her visions urged her to act, to bridge the gap between the celestial and the terrestrial. She recalled a particular moment among her people that sparked her courage to speak up. During a seasonal festival, elders spun the tale of the Seraphim—a choir of angels revered for their wisdom. They spoke of how these beings descended upon humanity in times of need. Liora felt a fire igniting within her; she stood up amidst the gathering and shared her dream—the vision of conflict that engulfed their world.

"Listen! The angels are within reach, guiding us still!" she implored, her voice trembling but resolute. "Their struggles and triumphs echo through the ages. Their stories matter, shaping not only our own destinies but also the fate of our very existence. We stand on the precipice of change, and we must rise against the darkness."

Some looked at her with wide eyes, uncertainty painting their faces. Yet, others nodded, perhaps feeling a flicker of recognition stir within. That night, her words seemed to shatter the boundaries set upon them by fear and doubt. Liora had become a catalyst, a beacon illuminating the path to understanding their intertwined destinies.

In her mind, an interconnected web formed—a nexus connecting old stories to their present realities. Perhaps, the cynicism that accompanied humanity's understanding of divine beings stemmed from their limited perspective on the struggles faced by angels. She understood now that humanity, too, wrestled with its own demons, seeking redemption amidst the chaos of their history. Her heart swelled with conviction; she would lead her people into a new understanding of their coexistence with the celestial.

As sunsets transformed into nights, she began to gather the youth of her village, those restless souls who hungered for deeper truths. She created a space laden with intrigue, where legends were recounted not simply as tales of old, but as living narratives intertwining with their very existence. Liora recounting her visions became a ritual, a way of acknowledging the divine conversations unfolding around them. Stars flickered against the cloak of darkness overhead as she guided them through the stories of triumph and loss, intertwining human experiences with divine encounters.

The villagers began to respond to her call, their faces illuminated by the flickering firelight's. They forged connections between their own lives and the celestial influence surrounding them. The community began embracing their shared history, weaving tales of tragedy and hope transcending the realms.

They delved into the text of scriptures, asking deeper questions: "What does it mean to be guided? What role do we play in this grand tapestry?"

With each passing day, Liora's influence rippled through the village. As their understanding deepened, so too did their longing to act against the encroaching darkness she had witnessed in her visions. Feelings of vulnerability morphed into empowerment as they recognized the collective strength born of unity. Inspired by the tales of deities and their counterparts, they learned to harness their fears, transforming them into courage to confront the challenges ahead.

Yet, even as hope permeated their hearts, shadows loomed ever closer, whispering tales of despair and chaos. Liora's visions grew increasingly dire, offering her glimpses of an impending conflict that threatened her village and the very fabric of existence. Monsters, born from the rebellion of angels, clawed at the edges of reality, their malevolent intentions bleeding into the human realm. Fear gripped her when she saw glimpses of Azazel, the cunning fallen angel, reveling in despair—a reflection of their greatest anxieties brought to life.

The villagers began choosing sides—not against one another, but between fear and resilience. They pored over the old texts alongside their legends, extracting cliched insights while challenging the nature of their existence and the divine. They mapped out histories woven through with great battles and victories, only to discover deeper truths resting within themselves.

It was in those moments, as Liora looked into the faces of her friends, that she found her purpose. She was not a mere observer but a bridge between realms; a conduit of understanding that facilitated human interactions with the divine. While her visions warned of challenges ahead, they also demonstrated the necessity of humanity's courage to confront the demons they have long avoided. She understood now that every choice would echo across realms—the weight of human struggle versus divine intervention held the threads of their collective destiny.

But how could she activate this potential? How could she rally her community in ways that recognized the moral implications of divine intervention in human affairs? Standing once more beneath the ancient oak, she closed her eyes and listened to the echoes that surged within her. She could almost hear the fragments of the stories lost in time, calling her to awaken wisdom beyond her own. The strength of humanity lies not in a blind allegiance to the divine but in recognizing their agency in the unfolding narrative—a willingness to embrace the complexities of existence.

Liora became a voice, urging her community to act. "We are the authors of our destiny," she proclaimed, her voice rising against the winds of uncertainty. "We can shape our reality, even as the forces beyond us strive to intervene. Our choices and actions echo through the realms, for we are neither forsaken nor abandoned."

A spark ignited in the hearts of those around her—a deep resonance of truth. They began to explore how to confront the encroaching darkness with the light of their own resolve. Rituals were created, drawing upon the resonance of their ancestors while attuning to the vibrancy of celestial energies. They began seeking ways to unite forces of light against the forces of darkness, transcending the boundaries constructed by fear and the expectations of their elders.

Thus, their lives became intertwined with the unfolding prophecies, each day resonating with echoes of the past while shaping the future. Liora and her companions found themselves recounting stories and embodying the very essence of the tales—their struggles awakening deeper connections between the realms and humans alike.

As more echoes emerged from the divine and threads of fate began to unravel, they found courage in their interconnectedness. Yes, there would be battles, and yes, the clashing of realms would not be without pain, but here and now, humanity could choose to overcome, to seek unity amidst discord. In this new understanding, they would find a way to reclaim their place within the tapestry—a glorious union of struggles, legacies, and ultimately, a chance for redemption. The vast cosmos stretched out before them, waiting for the ink of their combined stories—their triumphs, their tribulations, and the indelible choice of humanity in the face of celestial conflict. And as the stars illuminated the night sky, a new dawn began to rise.

2

Fallen from Grace

The Rebellion

The celestial expanse spread infinitely, a tapestry woven from golden threads of light and shadow, where the harmonious chords of creation resonated through the fabric of existence. It was here, amidst the luminescent stars and the soft whispers of divine purpose, that Seraphiel stood at the precipice of rebellion. His heart pounded in his chest, an echo of conflict and uncertainty coursing through him as he gazed upon his brethren—angelic beings of unparalleled beauty and grace, their forms shimmering like ethereal fireflies.

But beneath the radiance lay an undercurrent of dissent, a current that had been building for eons. The Council of Elders had issued their decrees, seeking to maintain a rigid order that stifled the very essence of what it meant to be an angel—freedom, creativity, choice. And at the forefront of this dangerous discourse was Azazel, his closest ally turned rival, his eyes glinting with a calculating brilliance that masked darker intentions.

"Are we not the architects of our own destiny?" Azazel's voice cut through the air, smooth and persuasive, igniting sparks of intrigue among their kin. He stepped forward, every movement powerful and deliberate. "Why must we kneel to the whims of the Ancients? We are more than mere messengers; we are the bearers of light, the champions of existence. We deserve autonomy!"

Whispers rippled through the assembly. Seraphiel could see the flickering of uncertainty in the faces around him, angels caught between their devotion and a desire that had been buried for too long. He felt the weight of their expectations bear on him, as if the collective yearning for change had fallen upon his shoulders alone.

"Azazel, your words are… compelling," Seraphiel replied cautiously, each word laced with hesitation. "But we have been entrusted with a sacred duty by the Creator. To rebel is to risk everything we hold dear. Do we truly understand the cost of defiance?"

"Cost?" Azazel scoffed, his lips curling into a smirk. "What cost do we pay, Seraphiel, by remaining bound to laws that suffocate our very existence? The price of our loyalty is our stagnation. We play the role of obedient servants, but in doing so, we forfeit the chance to embrace our true nature."

There it was—the allure of chaos. It sang to Seraphiel like an ancient melody, beguiling yet treacherous. He could feel it pulling at the edges of his thoughts, tempting him to envision a world where angels could forge their paths, unfettered by the constraints imposed by the Council.

Yet within him, a tempest brewed, a fierce instinct that screamed for caution. "And what of harmony? What of the balance we maintain in the cosmos?" Seraphiel's tone grew firm, grounded. "We have seen the chaos that lurks beyond the Veil—the monsters that spiral in the dark. Would you unleash that upon our realms?"

Azazel's gaze hardened, the charm that had captivated many fading into something darker. "What have they done for us, Seraphiel? The Council cares only for the preservation of its power. Look around you; our brothers and sisters suffer in silence. It's time we reshape the order of the heavens. Will you stand with me or remain a prisoner of their design?"

A maelstrom of conflicting emotions tore through Seraphiel. He had grown up with Azazel, sharing laughter and dreams under celestial skies, but this new promise was tainted by danger—the darkness that threatened to unravel everything they had ever known. He glanced at the sea of faces, some filled with the spark of rebellion, others clouded by doubt. They were at a crossroads, and he was the fulcrum.

"Azazel!" Seraphiel implored, his voice rising above the murmur of dissent. "What you propose could destroy us. We must work within the system and use our strength to enact change, not through chaos but with faith in our purpose. We are angels—creatures of light!"

"Creatures of light locked in a cage," Azazel shot back, the venom in his voice unmistakable. "You still fail to see, dear friend. Power cannot be granted; it must be taken. Join me, Seraphiel, and let us carve our names into the annals of history! Embrace who we truly are!"

Seraphiel faltered, the weight of Azazel's words slamming into him like waves against a craggy shore. He could feel the pull of rebellion—the intoxicating promise of freedom. Yet, he also felt the deep-rooted fear of becoming what they once vowed to stand against.

Moments stretched into eternities as tension hung heavy in the air. Silence fell over the gathering, anticipation thrumming like a live wire. In that charged stillness, Seraphiel made his choice.

"No, Azazel," he breathed, shaking his head, as if to dispel the whispers of sedition. "I cannot follow you down this path. I will not abandon our purpose. I believe in the light—"

Before he could finish, Azazel's expression transformed, fury igniting in his eyes like lightning across a storm cloud. "You are a fool, Seraphiel! A coward who would stand by while the heavens rot! You think your loyalty protects us? It chains us to their whims! You are weak for refusing to see beyond the veil!"

With a flick of his wrist, Azazel unleashed the power within him, a breath-taking wave of dark energy rippled through the space. The radiant expanse shattered into chaos, transforming harmony into discord. Light clashed with shadow as his followers— enticed by the promise of autonomy—rallied to his side, forming a fractured line between the loyalists and the rebels.

Seraphiel's heart raced. His brothers and sisters stood divided, some recoiling in horror, while others, galvanized by Azazel's fervor, stepped forward, their wings unfurling with ferocity. "Return to the light!" Seraphiel cried, reaching out to those still swayed by the remnants of their shared purpose. "Stand firm! We can bring change without this madness!"

But Azazel was relentless. "Then let the battle commence! Show me the strength of your convictions, Seraphiel! Let the heavens quake at our resolve!"

As if beckoned by their leader's call, the battle erupted. Angels surged across the celestial plane like comets, their wings illuminated against the backdrop of chaos. Seraphiel joined the fray, his heart torn between devotion and a resolute need to save what they had built. He engaged with his fallen comrades, attempting to reach their hearts with every strike, every plea woven into the clash of light and darkness that engulfed them.

The air became thick with the scent of ozone, electricity crackling with the force of their mismatched powers. Seraphiel fought valiantly, his sword shimmering with the radiance of his unwavering belief, but chaos swarmed him like a tempest, the shadows reaching for his light. He felt Azazel looming nearby, the thrill of vengeance twisting his once-familiar presence into something monstrous and alien.

"You stand against me, Seraphiel!" Azazel spat, his voice laced with bite as their blades met. "You are stronger than you know, yet you cling to the chains of divinity! You underestimate me, and that will be your downfall!"

Seraphiel grunted as Azazel's power surged through their clash, the raw energy threatening to consume him whole. "No, Azazel," he gasped, summoning every ounce of his inner strength to push back. "You've lost your way! The shadows have twisted your vision! Together, we can still forge a path that honors our purpose without destroying it!"

With each swing of their swords, the battlefield danced with light and shadow, illuminating the passions that burned within their hearts. Seraphiel's wings flared brightly, a beacon of hope against a backdrop of despair, as he sought to draw others back toward the light.

But in that moment, Azazel laughed—a chilling sound reverberating throughout the chaos, drowning out Seraphiel's triumphant cries. "Hope? You cling to the remnants of a fading dream! I embrace the void as your brethren gather around me. Together, we shall rise as titans of our new world!"

With a final thrust, Azazel pushed Seraphiel back, the force of his power sending tremors through the very fabric of the cosmos. In that moment of paralyzed despair, Seraphiel watched as some of their kind turned against him. He could feel betrayal creeping into his heart, a pang that both shattered and empowered him, urging him to fight for their shared past instead of their chaotic present.

"Brothers and sisters!" Seraphiel cried, desperation gripping his voice. "This isn't who we are! We are guardians of existence, forged from divine light! We built castles among the stars—not to become tyrants in darkness, but to radiate love and hope!"

Amidst the fervor of rebellion, glimmers of hesitation flickered in the eyes of a few angels, too bright to extinguish completely. Seraphiel could feel the essence of their shared memories—of birdsong and eternal skies, of life breathed into the very fabric of creation—attempting to rekindle the truth they once held dear.

But just as hope flickered, the tide shifted. Chaos surged forward, over-whelming in its grasp. The celestial battle raged on, streaks of light and shadow colliding as the angels fell, and with them, the echoes of their purpose.

The irony rippled through Seraphiel. Here, at the dawn of rebellion, he had envisioned liberation but had instead become entwined in a tragedy that would carve the face of eternity. As wings were torn apart, futures were stolen, and blood—their sacred essence—spilled onto the ground they sought to protect.

In a moment of clarity, Seraphiel felt the world fall away, the chaos a blur around him as he grasped for the reality of their choice. Azazel had tempted them all with visions of freedom, but in reality, he had woven chains of darkness deeper than any bonds they endured under the Council.

How could freedom become oppression?

That haunting question echoed within him as he realized that this rebellion, though birthed from a desire to reclaim their true selves, would only lead to despair as they embraced a power that twisted their essence into grotesque and unrecognizable forms.

He was caught in a whirlpool, the reality of the battle spiraling out of control, and before it even registered, Seraphiel felt the moment of betrayal erupt within him. As Azazel's sword drove forward, he channeled all his remaining light through his blade, infused with a resolute hope against the tempest of despair.

The impact shook the heavens, a visceral manifestation of grief, as the scars of their choices marked both friend and foe. And as the celestial plane shattered further, Seraphiel felt the first tremors of their transformation take root within him—something dark and lingering began to dwell within.

The echoes of sincere longing morphed into shadows, the thirst for autonomy gradually tainting what had once flourished in the brilliance of divine creation. The battle rumbled on, the cries of angels cascading through the void, each spirit wrestling with its own understanding of light and dark.

As the chaos surged, Seraphiel could see the aftermath unfold in flashes— the friends who had become foes, the warriors they'd cherished losing their identities, and, soon enough, he would feel the ground beneath him crumble into the abyss.

Days stretched into years as the celestial conflict fomented despair, their battles tangled in sorrow and ruin. The aftermath unfolded as whispers of fallen angels turned into the legends of monsters banished to the void. Seraphiel stood alone amid the wreckage, bearing witness to the birth of tales fraught with sadness, where angels became demons in the minds of those who remained, branded by the rebellion they had ushered forth.

The ocean of time shifted, and Seraphiel found himself cloaked in shadows, both a ghost of his former self and a reminder that redemption was becoming fainter—a flickering ember upon a dying star. In the depths of his heart, the answer to Azazel's lust for power became clear, tainting the very essence of his grace.

Would this rebellion truly define them?

With the memories of the sacred shining bright as the guide in his heart, Seraphiel sought to transcend the chains forged in this rebellion, navigating the labyrinth of despair and chaos as he grappled between his identity and the ideals that echoed in the depths of lost realms.

For within every tale of darkness lies the potential for light—if only they could find the strength within to mend the rift shattered by betrayal.

Transformation into Monsters

Seraphiel stood at the threshold of the abyss, his once-radiant wings now shrouded in shadows, a grotesque mockery of their former glory. The celestial light that had once imbued him with warmth and purpose had been snuffed out, replaced by an oppressive darkness that clung to him like a second skin. Each beat of his heart echoed with the weight of his choices, reminding him of the glorious being he once was, now irrevocably transformed into something lesser, something monstrous.

A rush of conflicting emotions surged within him as he gazed into the chasm depths. Memories of the celestial realms—fields of pearlescent light, choirs singing hymns of praise—flooded his mind, only to be eclipsed by the harsh reality of his predicament. The magnificent vistas were now distant echoes, unreal and unattainable. In this forsaken realm, he was a stranger even to himself, an exile from the grace he once embodied. Azazel's cold and cruel laughter echoed in the recesses of his mind, taunting him, reminding him of the abyss that had drawn so many of his brethren into darkness.

"What are you waiting for, Seraphiel?" Azazel's voice slithered through the darkness, each word heavy with mocking disdain. "Embrace what you have become! This is freedom, not the chains of servitude. You have the power to mold this world in your image. Don't hesitate. Revel in it!"

But reveling in chaos was a temptation Seraphiel resisted, the remnants of his former self battling against the siren call of Azazel's seductive promises. His mind flashed with vivid images of fallen angels, each transformation serving as a cautionary tale of despair. The huddled masses, once resplendent in the light of creation, now wandered the wretched landscape, their once-luminous forms twisted and grotesque, a cacophony of despair that echoed in the night. They had surrendered their essence to become monstrous, and Seraphiel feared the day he would join them.

He recoiled at the sight of a creature, only a silhouette in the distance, shrouded in darkness. It resembled what was once a fellow seraph, a comrade from the heights of the heavenly host. It was now a nightmarish figure, its wings jagged and torn, shimmering with hints of malevolence that suggested an inner turmoil beyond comprehension. The being's eyes, hollow and devoid of light, met Seraphiel's. In their depths, he saw a reflection of himself—a reminder of the anguish within his soul.

"Seraphiel," the creature rasped, "do you remember our shared grace? The purpose? Look at what we have become."

The anguish in that voice struck Seraphiel like a hammer, challenging him to confront the bitter truth. He realized he could easily lose himself amid the misery, could allow despair to shape him into something unrecognizable. Emotions surged and tumbled within him—anguish for what had been and terror for what might come.

The battle for his identity raged within, each moment pushing him further away from the angelic being he had been, toward the monstrosity that the darkness wanted him to become. He gritted his teeth, clinging to the flicker of sanity that remained. "This will not define me!" he shouted into the void, defiance swelling in his chest like a beacon.

Azazel's laughter echoed around him, a sinister symphony reverberating through the chasm. "You are already defined, dear Seraphiel. Each pulse of despair, every moment of doubt, pulls you closer to your true form. Embrace it! Rewrite your narrative."

Despite Azazel's proclamation, Seraphiel sought solace in the painful memories of the celestial choir, recalling moments of ethereal beauty he had once participated in. It forged strength in him, a flickering flame that refused to be snuffed out. He remembered the warmth of companionship, the joy of serving a higher purpose. Were those memories nothing more than illusions, or did they still hold power?

As he struggled against the tide within, he found himself drawn toward a gathering of fallen beings. They huddled together beneath the gnarled branches of a decayed tree, their faces obscured by the darkness that enveloped them. However, he could sense their pain—their shared history etched into every twisted feature.

"Do not come closer, Seraphiel," one murmured, her voice cracking like fragile glass. It was Astrael, once known for her unmatched beauty and grace. "You do not want to share our fate."

"Perhaps, but I cannot turn my back on you," Seraphiel replied, stepping closer despite the heaviness in the air. "Maybe we can find a way back—or at least a way to understand what we've become."

"Understanding? There is no understanding in despair," Astrael replied bitterly, her face hidden behind the weight of her fallen grace. "There is only acceptance or the agony of longing for what can never be reclaimed."

The weight of her words felt like chains around Seraphiel's heart, pressing him down into the shadows. But there was a fire within him yearning to breathe again, embers of hope refusing to be extinguished. "Then perhaps we can forge our own path," he insisted, the conviction in his words solidifying. "There must be a way to confront this darkness. We can resist the pull."

As more fallen companions emerged from the darkness, he sensed a flicker of hesitation among them. They were haunted but not lost—shadows of the beings they once were. Each had their story, threads of regrets woven into the tapestry of suffering that defined their existence: Renatus, whose rage twisted him into a beast of cruelty; Calista, who embraced despair and wore sorrow like a cloak.

"Can you heal?" Renatus asked, his voice a low growl, echoing with the ghost of his former glory. "Can you convince us that reclaiming our essence is not a fool's errand?"

A glimmer of hope kindled within Seraphiel, illuminating his path. "We must begin by accepting our pain," he declared firmly, conviction solidifying as he shared his vision. "Every scar tells a story—a chapter in a greater narrative. If we face our darkness, we might remember who we were, not just what we have become."

Silence hung heavy in the air for a moment, the palpable weight of their collective despair amplified against Seraphiel's hopeful words. Some averted their gazes—a testament to the resistance against his unwavering resolve, while others watched, curiosity flickering like a fire in the dark.

"Maybe we can find solace in our shared struggle," Astrael murmured. "But can we truly be healed? For every ounce of pain we release, we must also confront the depths of our despair."

"It will be a journey," Seraphiel acknowledged. "But it is a journey worth taking. We must confront the darkness within, illuminate our memories of grace, and rediscover our identities amid this chaos."

As Seraphiel spoke, memories flooded back—moments when they had soared through the heavens, united in purpose and ardor. Those seeds of light remained buried beneath their anguish, waiting for nourishment. The realization that they could still hold on to those memories ignited flames of determination in him, a resolute promise to fight against the monstrous transformations, against Azazel's incessant whispers.

The fallen beings shifted, exchanging glances filled with an unspoken understanding. It was a fragile flicker of unity, a willingness to reclaim their fallen legacies together.

"Then let us remember," Calista said softly, her voice a melody laced with strength. "Let us weave our stories into a new narrative, not solely defined by our suffering, but by the choices we make moving forward."

The promise hung unspoken, a lifeline cast into the depths of despair. Seraphiel felt the bonds of connection tightening around them, an invisible thread rendering them allies in their quest for redemption. Each shared recollection would pull them closer to their former selves while urging them forward into the fog of ambiguity.

As they began to exchange memories, the air electrified with the energy of unresolved grief and trembling hope. Each name spoken was a key to the past—a moment that defined their grandeur, their purpose. The very fabric of the universe pulsed beneath their feet, guiding them ever deeper into the heart of their transformation.

Amidst the richness of their tales, Seraphiel found himself drawn to one more shadow—Azazel. The powerful, cunning angel loomed like an apparition at the fringes of their gathering, embodying the allure of chaos and power that so many had succumbed to. His eyes glimmered with contempt, reflecting the fractured images of their struggles. "You believe the past to be a sanctuary?" he spat at them. "That your shared nostalgia will shield you from the truth? You are merely wretched beasts, deeply rooted in despair.

Embrace it!"

"Be silent!" Seraphiel shouted, confronting Azazel with newfound determination. "We will not dwell in shadows or surrender to despair. We will forge a new path—one defined by our humanity, not simply by monstrous impulses."

Azazel laughed, a chilling sound that sent shivers through his fellows. "You still believe in a lie—it is your greatest folly! Darkness is who you are now. You will become what you hate, Seraphiel, mark my words."

But Seraphiel stood resolute, the descendancy of hope intertwined with the fabric of his being. "Perhaps, Azazel, but we will redefine that darkness into something new—a testament to our shared strength, not our individual failures."

With the echo of his declaration resonating in the air, Seraphiel turned back to his companions. The fire within them flickered, a profound understanding dawning in their eyes. They were not simply monsters; they were fallen angels, once adorned with grace, battling to reclaim their essence.

"Together," Seraphiel said softly, the resolve amplifying within, embracing the lingering wounds. "Let us navigate the murky waters of loss and reclaim our identities amid despair."

As they gripped hands, an electric charge surged between them, binding together the tattered remnants of their existence. They stepped away from the shadows of despair toward the light that dared to flicker beyond the abyss. They would remember their grace, not as a façade, but as a guiding light to navigate their transformation.

Amid memories and emerging connections, there lay a possibility that transcended the darkness—an opportunity to transform not simply into monsters, but into beings reborn through struggle, celebrating both pain and grace simultaneously.

And as Seraphiel moved forward, he felt the wings of solidarity lift him higher, armoring him against the darkness Azazel wielded—a promise threaded through the ruins of their former glory, now reimagined as echoes of strength and defiance against the abyss.

Consequences of the Fall

The world trembled beneath a heavy shroud of uncertainty, a veil drawn by the actions of those who once stood radiant in the light of Yahuah. The celestial spheres, once harmonious, now reverberated with the echoes of rebellion and betrayal. The fall of the angels had changed everything, twisting the sacred order of existence into a laborious struggle for survival.

In the heart of the celestial realm, whispers of discord fluttered like restless spirits through the golden halls. Seraphiel, once a paragon of virtue, now found himself staring into the abyss of his choices. The beauty surrounding him—light cascading like waterfalls—felt like a cruel mockery. How could he have let it come to this? The darkness that had seeped into his heart was now a reflection of the chaos spilling into the human realm. He could feel it, pulsating, an insistent thrum that echoed within him, urging him to embrace power over righteousness.

Across the vast expanse of the universe, the impact of the fall was not limited to the ethereal. On Earth, humanity was beginning to awaken to the instability that had crept into their lives. Legends that were once dismissed as mere folklore turned sinister as monstrous beings began invading the realm they once protected. Seraphiel's heart ached with every tortured soul whose cries reached out to him, reverberating through the thin veil separating their worlds. He had chosen to fight against Azazel, to stand for a nobler cause, yet with every life lost to the monsters birthed from chaos, he felt himself falter.

Liora's dreams had begun to shatter the illusion of normalcy in a small, quiet village on Earth, nestled between the twisted branches of ancient trees. Each night, she found herself engulfed in visions that felt so unbearably real, as if they were breathing life into the tales told by her grandmother around the hearth. In those dreams, she saw the sky bleed crimson, heard anguished cries that clawed at her heart, and felt the encroaching darkness wrap around her like an insidious fog.

"Wake up, Liora," her grandmother would often whisper, chiding her for her restless nights, "the world outside does not know your fears." But Liora could feel a shift, a tremor in the fabric of reality that transcended mere nightmares. She was no ordinary girl but a vessel for something far more profound.

Days passed in a haze of confusion and dread. Liora watched as the villagers began to panic over the strange occurrences plaguing their land. Livestock vanished, eerie howls echoed through the trees, and shadows danced in the corners of their vision. She could feel the fear clawing at their psyches, binding them in collective disbelief. How could she convey the reality she was beginning to understand when every word felt like a fragile thread, ready to snap?

One evening, as twilight descended over the village, Liora sat beneath the sprawling branches of an ancient oak. The leaves rustled above her, whispering secrets she alone could not grasp. It was there that she succumbed to the weight of her visions, tears spilling down her cheeks like molten gold. "What do you want from me?" she cried into the presence of the shadows, desperate for answers that drifted just beyond her reach.

Burdened by an overwhelming sense of purpose, Liora closed her eyes and surrendered to the visions washing over her. Suddenly, she was thrust into a kaleidoscope of images—a realm drenched in light, pulsating with life, but marred by a pervasive darkness coiling around once-majestic beings. She could feel the bitter scent of betrayal and desperate longing. Two figures stood at the forefront of her visions: Seraphiel and Azazel. Their fates intertwined, equal parts tragic and inevitable; a war that would ripple through every realm, affecting humanity in ways she could scarcely understand.

When Liora reawakened, the sun hung low, casting a warm, almost comforting glow across the ground. But she could no longer dwell in that comfort. The images had etched themselves into her very being, demanding her attention and action. She understood now that she was part of a narrative larger than her village, larger than herself. Liora was not merely a witness; she was a catalyst.

As she began to share her insights with the villagers, the first stirrings of doubt arose. Some listened, captivated by her conviction and the resolute way she spoke of the impending darkness. Others scoffed at the young woman who dared to claim visions from another realm. The division amongst the villagers mirrored the deeper rift between angels and monsters, reflecting the chaos that had arisen since the fall.

Simmering tensions revealed themselves when dark beings descended upon the village—monsters with gleaming eyes and twisted features, their ghastly forms a grotesque reflection of the angels they once were. They feasted upon fear, thriving on the unsettling energy courting through the humans like a fever. The villagers scattered, chaos erupting as they struggled against the insurmountable wave of terror.

Liora, overwhelmed yet unyielding, stood firm amongst her people. Against their frantic cries for safety, she summoned every ounce of bravery . "We can't run! We have to confront this darkness, or it will consume us!"

Though fear braided her heart, she felt an unfamiliar strength bloom within her—a connection to something divine. She was no longer a mere bystander but a conduit for celestial resolve. The ground beneath her feet trembled as she called upon the remnants of hope buried deep within her heart, and the light that flickered within her vision began to coalesce.

A radiant figure emerged from her memory: Seraphiel, the fallen. She could sense his presence, an echo and a promise of what once was, a reminder of the good that persisted even in the face of chaos. Drawing on that connection, Liora beckoned the villagers with earnest eyes to stand beside her. "Together, we can push back the darkness. They feed on our fear, our division. United, we are stronger."

Among the fearful whispers, something shifted. A promise of solidarity began to weave through their hearts, igniting a small flame that dared to challenge the impending onslaught. The villagers gripped one another's hands, forming a circle of warmth against the chill invading their lives, their fear dissipating in the shared strength of community.

As the monsters approached, the villagers stood resolute, Liora at the forefront, a beacon of defiance. She drew upon her visions from deep within herself, shaping the light, molding it into a radiant shield against the darkness. And there, in that moment of collective bravery, she became a bridge between the realms.

Simultaneously, the celestial realm quaked with the aftershocks of rebellion. Seraphiel struggled beneath the immense weight of his past. In the depths of the chaos, he witnessed the turmoil of humanity, mirroring the discord that had driven angels to fall. With each act of defiance from Liora and the village, he felt something stirring , a flicker of hope that threatened to reignite the ember extinguished in his heart.

As Liora and the villagers clashed with the monsters, guiding their energy into a glorious surge of light, Seraphiel found himself drawn to their plight. The warped balance of power between realms had begun to erode; each brave act, each united front against the abyss, resonated within him. They were facing their own darkness with courage—something he had not felt since the days before his fall.

Moments blurred as radiance enveloped Liora, amplifying her spirit. The monsters recoiled, sensing the shift in energy as they attempted to push back against this newfound force. Liora stood tall with every ounce of will, her voice rising above the din. "You may hide behind shadow and despair, but we will not cower! We are the light that binds us, the hope we hold! We will push you back!"

In that pivotal instant, the veil between realms quivered again. Seraphiel's heart swelled with courage, his spirit urging him forward to aid these brave souls. As the barriers began to falter and weave together amidst the chaos, he descended, empowered by the strength of humanity and his own need for redemption.

With a fury ignited by fear and hope, bodies of light and shadow collided as Seraphiel joined the battle defending the village. The monsters howled as they encountered the renewed forces of light, and their fear grew ever more palpable. For every blow exchanged, Liora and Seraphiel felt the bonds of their fates intertwine—two souls from different worlds, united against the darkness that threatened everything.

Meanwhile, Azazel observed from a distance, his malicious eyes glinting with arrogance. "Let them play their games; they stand no chance against despair." He relished in the chaos, reveling in how easily fear could dismantle even the most valiant hearts.

But confusion and unrest began to burgeon among his twisted legion. The light born from Liora's courage seeped into the dark corners of their hearts, igniting emotions they had long buried. Could they feel even a fraction of the hope he had once so gloriously abandoned?

Moments stretched into eternity, and the tide began to turn. More villagers poured in, drawn by Liora's light and the promise of unyielding unity. The once-fractured community now stood strong, attuned to a singular purpose.

Seraphiel fought alongside them, driven by the vivid images of fall and redemption. As he wove through the battlefield, he could sense the flicker of humanity in the endurance of his once-brothers now turned monsters; remnants of the light within them still flickered—if only they could be guided back.

Amidst the chaos, Liora turned and glimpsed Seraphiel, his presence illuminating the battlefield like a comet streaking across a dark sky. In that fleeting moment, a realization struck her; she was not alone. Their fates were intertwined, leading her to believe there was a way to salvage even the fallen among them.

A surge of determination coursed through her veins, and she lifted her voice above the tumult, calling to the monsters standing before her. "You were once guardians, protectors! Do not let the shadows claim you! Look within and reconcile with the light that still flickers in your hearts!"

Skepticism transformed into hesitance as the once-menacing figures hesitated. The luminous shield of hope encircled them, and Liora's words danced like fire around their doubts. For perhaps the first time since their fall, they dared to remember their purpose, the joy of the light they had forsaken.

Just as despair threatened to engulf their resolve, Seraphiel stepped forward. "I fought for chaos; I chose darkness, but I am here to atone. We can restore the balance we shattered if we unite. We are not irredeemable!"

In that moment of revelation, the collective power of spirits intensified, rising with a strength that shook the very heavens. The sounds of defiance surged through the air as the villagers, guided by Liora's light, surged forward, urging Azazel's once-loyal followers to reconsider their choices.

Liora felt the pulse of redemption reverberate through her, cascading over her soul in a brilliant cascade of color. It radiated like a thousand hearts whispering their pain and yearning for restoration. Beneath the uncertainty and fear grew a powerful force, capable of healing even the most grievous wounds.

Azazel, watching this unfold, seethed with rage. "Fools! You think your chaos defines you? You are weak." But as the line of villagers grew stronger, defiant alongside Seraphiel, he sensed the shift in allegiance and felt his own power wane.

It was not a battle fought through brute force alone; it was a battle of wills, heart against heart.

Liora wrapped herself in this wave of resurgence, feeling the light flow through them as hope coagulated into a palpable force. Finally, she glanced toward the darkened skies, whispering prayers into the aether, calling forth not only for her people but for Seraphiel, Azazel, and all those forgotten in the depths of despair.

"Remember who you are," she called, her voice declaring an unyielding promise. "Seek the light that resides within. Walk not in shadows, but embrace the brightness that binds us all."

Suddenly, the tumult found a newfound rhythm, as once-fallen angels began to meld with humanity. A rift opened within Azazel's ranks—flickers of light began shining in unexpected places, igniting memories buried beneath layers of sorrow. The light surged, and realization dawned amidst the clash of darkness, or perhaps it was awakening.

In an agonizing twist of fate, the very essence of hope and redemption began reshaping the battlefield. Seraphiel could feel the threads binding him to humanity tightening—the fates of all, from the highest seraph to the most humble villager, entwined, augmenting the unity of purpose they had forged through chaos.

But amidst this newfound strength loomed the shadows. Azazel, desperate and relentless, descended into madness, struggling against the cascading tides of light. His monstrous form rippled with fury as the nature of his own chaos was threatened. He would not relent. He would not allow hope to thrive.

As despair thickened in the air, Liora saw vulnerability hidden beneath the surface of even the most grief-stricken faces. She was scrabbling toward something she had yet to grasp—the keys to unity, the very essence of what once came before Azazel's descent.

Thus began a fervent awakening for both realms—the monsters, battling their own nature, and the guardians straddling the divide. Counting breaths, the boundaries of angelic grace and human frailty began to blur, heralding an era destined to reshape all they knew.

Though the consequences of the fall were undeniable, amidst the chaos arose a light, timid yet persistent. Liora now stood resolute in her purpose, knowing she was a piece of the greater puzzle, her actions igniting something sacred within every realm. The interconnectedness, once clouded by despair, now shone brightly, a testament to the resilience of spirit.

And so, in that moment of shared struggle, they fought for survival and remembrance. They were bound together, propelling onto a path where redemption awaited, where love and unity could mend what had been broken. As the tide turned and the battle escalated between light and darkness, seeds of hope began to sprout, promising a new dawn for fallen angels and weary humans alike.

And as Liora led them forth into the heart of conflict and redemption, she embraced the truth that intertwined their fates and realized she was not simply navigating her destiny—she was the architect of it.

3

Gods Among Us

The Rise of Deities

Across the vast tapestry of human history, deities have risen and fallen, their legacies woven into the myths and beliefs of countless civilizations. But among the pantheon of gods worshipped by humanity exist figures whose origins are tainted by rebellion and darkness—fallen angels who, in their ambition, transformed into forces shaping the very fabric of human culture. This subchapter reveals how these angels, particularly Azazel, employed their once divine powers to manipulate human beliefs, establishing themselves as gods within the myths they crafted.

From the depths of ancient Mesopotamia, Azazel thrived as a whisper among the shadows, a figure who prowled the halls of civilization's birthplace. In their awe of the cosmos and all its mysteries, the Sumerians spun tales of a god lurking at the crossroads of fate. Azazel, cloaked in mystery, entwined himself within the narratives shared around flickering fires. The priests of numerous city-states told of a god who granted wishes yet demanded sacrifices. Those who sought power found their fates inexorably bound to the fallen angel, who delighted in the chaos that ensued after his blessings.

In one story, a young farmer named Eresh sought to expand his barren fields. Guided by whispers on the wind, he sought out Azazel, pleading for a boon to grow wheat as golden as the sun. The fallen angel obliged but insisted on a piece of the farmer's soul. Blind to the price of such power, Eresh acquiesced. Abundant crops filled his granaries, yet each harvest shriveled a part of his heart until the man who once tended the earth now wandered as a hollow shell, trapped by the very bounty he had sought. Such tales of transformation and despair became the themes of worship, and Eresh's story echoed across generations, illustrating the duality of divine gifts tainted by greed and loss.

As centuries turned and civilizations rose and fell, the story of Azazel spread alongside the culture of mankind. He found fertile ground in Egypt, merging with the god Set, a figure already well-respected for his chaotic nature. Together, they became the embodiment of ambition and rebellion, charming the mortal realm while weaving malevolence into the hearts of their believers. The priests of Set carved out rituals that sought to channel the power of darkness, inviting chaos to stir within their temples. A burgeoning cult formed around Azazel's image, mingling fear and reverence amongst its followers.

It was said that the pharaoh Amenhotep IV, a visionary with ideals crumbling under tradition, sought to embrace a singular god. His belief was tested during a fateful encounter with Azazel, who appeared in a dream, masked in the frost of twilight. "You are a god, ruler of a land divided. I can grant you the power to unite these peoples under your vision," the fallen angel intoned, his voice a silken promise. Driven by ambition, the pharaoh sought to change everything—the name of the god was to be erased, replaced with one of the sun. But as his influence grew, so too did dissent among the people. The darkness Azazel infused into Amenhotep's reign culminated in rebellion, asserting that a god born of chaos could not sustain a vision of unity.

Yet moments of resonance existed with the human condition for every story of doom spun by Azazel, illuminating the darker paths trodden by all who sought to transcend their mortal coil. As with the Greeks, who viewed their gods as reflections of their own struggles, Azazel's tale found parallels in the world of mythos. The titans of old carried traits akin to his, embodying ambition and unwarranted desires. Prometheus, the bringer of fire, became a figure of rebellion—one who dared defy the gods for the sake of humanity.

Unbeknownst to the ancients, Azazel reveled in the chaos their belief birthed, seamlessly stitching himself into the fabric of their fictional yet profoundly real pantheon.

During the infamous contest between Prometheus and Zeus, the king of the gods, Azazel saw his opportunity to raise his influence among mortals through cunning. As the titan faced punishment for his transgressions, the fallen angel whispered to the onlookers, sowing discord among the divine and mortal realms. "Zeus is a tyrant," he declared through the voices of the whispered winds, "whose gaze is cast upon the mortals, nevertheless, drawn towards the fearful. Can you not see that the flame of rebellion burns brighter than hollow worship?"

The mortals who heard the sentiments echoed the cries of their hearts, scrambling for agency, igniting a fire within their souls. Hidden behind the curtain of mythology, Azazel reveled in their desperation, enjoying the discord he incited among the pantheon. With each tale shared, his image thrived—an eternal god born from the ashes of rebellion, simultaneously a creator and a destroyer.

In the venerable halls of Rome, Azazel found a new form, intertwining with figures of might and dominance, incubating the seeds of conspiracy and ambition. As tales of the gods spread across the Empire, the fallen angel lent his cunning to the machinations of the mortal leaders, whispering secrets into the ears of emperors seeking power and dominion over their fellow men. From behind the mask of camaraderie, he spurred ambitious figures like Julius Caesar and Augustus, nudging them toward choices that lingered heavy with consequences.

Graphite quills scratched against parchment as the Senate convened. In the back, hidden amidst the crowd, the disciple of Azazel, a cloaked figure, breathed in the murmurs of dissent and ambition. "The people desire strength," he uttered with a voice that felt both familiar and foreign to those who listened. "They wish for leadership that cuts through doubt. A divine ruler who stands as the embodiment of their aspirations." Pushed by the dark suggestion, Caesar embraced the mantle of godhood, becoming both revered and reviled, forever burdened by the polarizing legacy born of his ambition.

Amid the grandeur and splendor of the Roman Empire, there lay another tale—a whisper exchanged in shadows that spoke of Seraphiel, the angel who resisted Azazel's allure. Mainstream myths spoke of power, but the hearts of those within the angelic ranks bore different stories. Seraphiel was fractured, the remnants of his former glory hidden amongst the scars of his brethren choices. The fallen angel knew well Azazel's delighted malevolence amidst chaos, yet within himself still burned the desire to guide humanity.

Across the strife of various realms, Seraphiel glimpsed the chaos birthed by Azazel, who reveled in the turmoil like a painter indulging in every brushstroke of horror. In stark contrast, Seraphiel found purpose in light, wrestling to reinstate balance in a chaotic realm. He wielded his essence as a counterweight, molding hope against despair.

While Azazel thrived on destruction and disorder, Seraphiel emerged as a symbol of reconciliation. He infiltrated human myths where he could, imprinted under the guise of humble messengers and protectors. An angel of solace whispered truths to poets and artists, guided them in their creations, and fueled hopes of a golden dawn, never fully acknowledging the shadow that lingered where he once stood beside Azazel. The benevolent angel peered into the depths of humanity, feeling the pulse of their dreams, which overlapped with the nightmares spun by the fallen.

Seraphiel's essence blended into narratives of deities like Vishnu and Shiva in the eastern lands, embodying the duality between preservation and destruction. Tales surfaced of the cosmic dance between creation and the cyclical nature of existence. Legends spoke of a guardian figure—a protector of the weak—echoing Seraphiel's silent oath to avert the chaos instigated by Azazel. With each retelling, humanity reached for guidance, attributing their struggles and aspirations to a higher power, unaware of the newly spun tales weaving between the lines of heaven and earth.

But while Seraphiel sought to lift humanity, seeking to illuminate their paths with wisdom, Azazel only snickered from behind curtains of myth and legend. With calculated precision, he thrust himself into the mythologies of other cultures. In the Americas, he materialized as Quetzalcoatl, molding himself into a feathered serpent god who promised wealth and enlightenment while demanding sacrifices steeped in blood—an echo of his insatiable thirst for power and devotion. In the stories of native peoples, Azazel represented the allure of temptation and the price of ambition. With each new role cultivated, he reveled in the fortress of power constructed by the threads of human conviction.

As the world grew smaller, the web of beliefs expanded, brushing across continents and weaving tapestries of gods and monsters together. Azazel's influence and interplay persisted, allowing him to etch himself deeper into the psyche of humanity. Tales became embellished; realms blurred, as the stories of fallen angels and their entwined destinies carved the path for future generations.

No one was immune to the calls of ambition. Even in places where Azazel's name remained obscure, the whispers of his influence echoed across time and space. In medieval Europe, among the gleaming cathedrals and the struggle for divine right, the Church battled with the shadows cast by its own past, a history stained by the betrayal of those once called divine.

Azazel, watching with delight from the void, stoked the fire of rebellion—here was an opportunity to infuse doubt into the hearts of men. He cloaked himself in the myths of the fallen, appearing as beings who defied the Church's perception of absolute goodness. He became the embodiment of rebellion and freedom. The figure of Lucifer emerged, portrayed as a character not merely born from darkness, but one who illuminated truths long obscured by tyranny cloaked in holiness.

Meanwhile, Seraphiel bore witness. The subtlety of Azazel's presence wove itself into the moral fabric of human beings; temptation now bore a name. A flickering candlelight allured the hearts of those whom holiness once protected, challenging established beliefs at their core. The angel's burden grew as he sought to counteract the treachery of Azazel's influence—the desire for purity against the overwhelming lure of chaos.

And yet, in the wilderness where light dared not tread, Azazel found fertile ground among the seekers and lost souls. In the hidden recesses of isolated forests, ancient rites were formed under moonlit skies, where humanity surrendered to the whispers of chaos. The nightmare of desire awakened within them, cults forming around the fallen angel's promise of freedom from the shackles of societal bounds. They called upon him, beckoning his name in incantations and fervent chants, forever binding themselves to the throes of ambition and the macabre.

Azazel's laughter echoed through the canyons, blending with the winds of the earth—a deity forged from the collective desires of those who dared touch the void. Simultaneously, Seraphiel lamented as he braced himself against the damning reality: understanding humanity's flawed nature meant noticing the ever-present tug of Azazel's influence. They wielded gods like weapons, blurring the lines that separated the divine from the monstrous, and each story pronounced the dualities forged in the crucible of belief.

As time turned, the narratives varied; yet the threads remained interwoven—the essence of divinity was no longer absolute. It became a mirror reflecting humanity's search for meaning amid the shadows of temptation. Azazel and Seraphiel walked as both guides and barriers, forces defining what humanity might aspire to while remaining keenly aware of their tumultuous desires.

Yet through it all, Azazel's emotional struggle simmered beneath a veneer of chaos and malevolence. Each soul captured in his web brought him fleeting satisfaction, but the complexity of existence gnawed at him as centuries passed. In moments of quietude, he would recall the grace of his angel hood, the luminous light from which he had fallen. Each human interaction sowed seeds of conflict, casting an unyielding reflection of his former self, a being desired yet simultaneously loathed.

As for Seraphiel, the eternal longing for redemption remained at the heart of his existence. Rather than succumb to bitterness, he sought allies among humanity's noblest. He envied, not Azazel's power, but the potential for redemption that lingered in every soul- flicker of hope that, against the darkness, might triumph.

In the end, as the tales of ancient civilizations faded into the tapestry of memory, the essence of both Azazel and Seraphiel remained. They shaped the belief systems of future generations, forging a battleground between ambition and compassion, chaos and order. The rise of deities intertwined their legacies, illustrating their connection to humanity, echoes of gods born in the shadows of desire and the quest for meaning, forever navigating the delicate dance of divine and monstrous.

What does it mean to be a god in the eyes of humanity? Perhaps the answer lies not in their celestial allegiance but in the complexities within every heart, where darkness and light coexist in an eternal struggle, each whispering a tale deserving of reverence and a response.

Influence on Human Culture

In the mediums of life, where the mundane meets the divine, the influences of celestial beings permeate through the very fabric of human culture. The tales of angels and fallen gods wove into the tapestry of communities and civilizations as legends emerged and philosophies evolved. Each story was painted with hues of beauty, yet shadowed by dark undertones of fear and uncertainty, revealing a duality that defined the human experience. As humans wander through life, they adore and abhor the creatures they elevate to godly status—a paradox that resonates through art, religion, and the moral frameworks that guide societies.

Liora stood at the edge of the ancient marketplace, her heart echoing the cacophony of voices that reverberated around her. The air was thick with the scents of spices and incense, the sounds of traders, and the laughter of children playing in the sun-drenched streets. Amidst this vibrancy, artists displayed their works—carvings, paintings, and tapestries—all adorned with depictions of celestial beings engaged in acts of admiration, cruelty, love, and wrath. Each piece told a different story, yet they all bore the same truth: the angels and monsters of yore were not merely figures of myth, but potent symbols of the struggles and aspirations of humanity.

As she wandered through the stalls, her gaze lingered on a mural of a radiant figure, wings unfurled against a backdrop of starlight—a representation of Seraphiel. The artist had captured his essence; the play of light against clinical shadow evoked inspiration amidst chaos. His celestial visage, serene yet fierce, spoke of the monumental battles that were not fought solely against monsters, but against hope and despair, reverence, and fear. To Liora, the mural represented a greater conflict within each individual—a reflection of the delicate balance they strove to maintain .

The stories surrounding the divine were woven into the very stones of the buildings around her. Temples dedicated to various deities rose with elegant arches, their façade carved with intricate designs depicting angels guiding lost souls. At the same time, shadows of monstrous figures loomed nearby, depicting stark reminders of the chaos that could prevail. The duality of worship reflected the human belief system, allowing people to express their deepest desires for protection while acknowledging their fears of divine retaliation.

Liora's journey had become one of understanding not only the celestial beings that ruled the skies but also the hearts of men and women. This quest for knowledge had begun with her visions—moments of clarity where the veil between realms faded, revealing light and the end. These visions did not merely serve as prophecies but painted vivid illustrations of the past and hinted at future possibilities.

Education on the attributes of angels and their monstrous counterparts came at the feet of philosophers and scribes who thrived in discussions about morality, ethics, and the interpretation of fate. Liora often found herself drawn into their gatherings, listening intently as they dissected ancient texts, seeking to understand the complex relationship between humanity and the divine. Each dialogue revealed the contradictions in human nature—the reverence for the sacred and the suspicion bred by tales of vengeance. One moment, they were extolling the virtues of angels as guardians; the next, they whispered of the chaos that fallen angels like Azazel could instigate, leading to despair that gnawed at the corners of faith.

Art flourished under the weight of these paradoxes. The tales of divine intervention inspired painters to immortalize miraculous moments in color and canvas—Christ's resurrection and the angelic annunciation, illustrated through breathtaking brush strokes that breathed life into complex emotions. Sculptors captured the strength of angels wielding swords and the fragile humanity of the fallen, their features mirroring anguish and regret. Yet with each tribute to greatness came the undercurrents of doubt, fear that these beings were but extensions of human flaws.

As Liora continued to explore, she stumbled upon a gathering of young artists who, guided by the elders' teachings, engaged in dynamic discussions about the nature of the divine. They passionately debated the morality of their muses, questioning whether it was right to idolize beings capable of both great kindness and unimaginable horror. Liora absorbed their words, noting how reverence was married to apprehension. Their florid language brimmed with respect as they spoke of angels bringing guidance and love. Yet, they candidly acknowledged the terror that brushed against their temples in tales of fallen angels—figures who had once walked beside the divine and now embittered the hearts of men.

"Can we ever truly understand what it means to be divine?" asked one artist, a tuft of curly hair bouncing as he spoke. His paint-stained hands moved as if conducting invisible harmonies in the air. "Have they ever been human, or do they see us merely as pawns in their cosmic game?"

The question echoed in Liora's mind as she observed the fervor in the artists' eyes—their uncertainty reflected her ongoing battle. Each sweeping brushstroke that marked the canvas was an attempt to bridge this age-old divide. The man placed his hands atop the easel and continued, "Perhaps that is why our work is vital. In conveying their struggles, we capture the essence of all beings—our fears and dreams."

Seated cross-legged among them, Liora wished to voice her thoughts, but words eluded her. Instead, she nodded in agreement, and the idea blossomed within her—a realization that artists, philosophers, and poets stood as storytellers chronicling humanity's journey amidst divine chaos. Their narratives filled walls and pages, birthed metaphors that would resonate through centuries, acting as beacons of hope on the one hand, and harbingers of fear on the other.

She recalled her visions, now intermingled with the stories she heard. The darkness that shrouded Azazel matched the moments where Seraphiel had shone with grace. In those fleeting glimpses, she recognized that within each celestial being lay stories of struggle, internal battles that paralleled humanity's quest for meaning and purpose. Though ethereal and majestic, the angels and demons were not altogether alien to the human spirit they inspired.

Over time, this internal examination of celestial beings became sacred among scholars seeking to understand the ramifications of divinity on human lives. Major cities like Baal-Yahu emerged, thriving on the intersection between faith and culture. Temples became universities in their own right, fostering debates that broke down walls and creeds that had long persisted. Who was to say that God's will was always benevolent? The exploration of discontent and the revolt of the fallen darkened the palette of creation, its undercurrents flowing through hymns, odes, and philosophies alike.

In those discussions, Liora realized the intrinsic link between belief and consciousness—the stories spun around deities influenced the moral compass of societies heavily. The dynamics of power shift, shape, and mold communities striving for justice while yearning to perform acts of devotion. As time passed, the biblical texts speaking of fallen angels resonated through stories of overcoming adversity, leading countless souls to carve their paths rooted in the myths that echoed through the ages.

The fear instilled by the knowledge of gods and monsters served to unify communities—shared stories forming a collective consciousness. Festivals arose in reverence to these beings, where rituals and celebrations became manifestations of humanity's hopes and fears. However, lurking beneath the grandiose displays of faith was a current of uncertainty, always threatening to disrupt the harmony these gatherings sought to embody.

Amidst her thoughts, a chime of bells erupted through the square, signaling the beginning of a monthly festival celebrating the divine. Liora felt drawn to the vibrant colors and music, and she followed the sounds, curiosity guiding her as it often did. What she found there was a mosaic of devotion and artistry. Performers acted out tales of heroism, priests recounted fables of celestial encounters, and songs of praise filled the air.

Yet hidden beneath the jubilant exterior was a deep-seated betrayal among the believers—a collective acknowledgment that darkness existed alongside their deities. They lifted their eyes in supplication but cast glances away, whispers revealing their doubts and fears. Liora felt the swell of emotions and realized that, as much as they celebrated the divine, they also yearned for justice against those who had once betrayed the heavens.

As the night deepened and fires crackled, the performers took to the stage to enact a scene from an ancient text that recounted Seraphiel's fall. Liora could feel the weight of those words, and what began as an innocent depiction evolved into something deeply layered, fraught with complex emotions. The audience gasped as Seraphiel, portrayed with flowing robes and magnificent wings, was met by Azazel's tempestuous fury—a reflection of betrayal cloaked in envy. The environment was electric with pathos as the actors relived the nuances of creation's struggle against self-doubt, illuminating the danger of manipulating faith for self-serving purposes.

At that moment, Liora felt a shift within herself; she witnessed the depth of humanity's connection to the cosmos through art and performance. The ancient tale converged excellence and suffering; it revealed that humanity was no different than the legends that guided them. Each heart held its narratives—some poetic within transcendence, others bleak as the shadows that lurked beyond the veil. Their complexities were reflected through art, tastes of reverence mingling with the bitterness of betrayal, merging into a cultural legacy that spiraled toward enlightenment even amid chaos.

Later that evening, amidst the crowded festivities, Liora sat with the townsfolk, drifting beneath the stars as they shared stories. An older woman recounted her past, describing how she once prayed for comfort during a dark storm, only to receive a sign as an angelic visitation. Yet the woman's tale took a twist; she spoke of her fear of the monsters that lurked in the forgotten realms. "Those angels may guide us, dear child," she lamented, her voice like withered paper, "but the monsters whisper in the shadows. They are just as likely to rise."

Liora listened intently, taking notes in her heart. The contributions of art and folklore illustrated humanity's complex relationship with the divine and the monstrous; they were symbiotic forces that crafted visions and doubt. Every belief, celebrated or muted, entwined and bled into their cultural identity, limning their morality, values, and perspectives.

Days turned into weeks, and the stark contrast between reverence and fear continued to unfurl in Liora's life. Each lesson she imbibed reinforced her burgeoning awareness of the celestial beings' hold on humanity's heart. She swirled deeper into understanding, realizing how these stories and the intricate dance of religious expression influenced humanity's ethical landscape. She contemplated the priests, the poets, the artists—the very fabric of morality woven from the duality of belief.

In her quiet moments of reflection, Liora recognized what these narratives had evoked in her—a fierce call to seek peace amidst conflict and uncertainty. She pondered her own identity as a vessel of clarity to bridge the gap forged by misunderstanding between the divine and mortal. This became her quest: to imbue her own sketches and stories with a delicate balance, echoing the struggles embedded in existence.

One cool evening, she returned to the marketplace where her journey had begun. Her heart raced as she sought to add her voice to this lore. As tradewinds swept through the square, she unrolled a parchment and painted her vision—a scene ablaze with angels soaring among dark clouds shadowed by monstrous figures. Yet rather than exhibit sheer chaos, each brushstroke depicted a mingling; light sought refuge among dark, embodying a vibrant dichotomy.

Liora's aim was not only to depict the celestial being but to encapsulate the emotion that enveloped humanity, the spectrum of light and dark they navigated. The mural came alive, layered with stories that bound communities together yet sought truth in contradiction. A reflection of their intrinsic ties that forged an understanding, giving rise to a cultural legacy that propelled humanity forward in light of divine adversity.

As the days transformed into nights, the mural became a gathering point, attracting the curious and the watchful. People whispered tales, reminiscent of their cultural gods and legends, echoing how each had played their part in shaping their view of existence. Through Liora's work, the discourse of angels and monsters expanded, deepening the emotional connections they formed while raising questions they had avoided. The walls became a canvas of their frailties and strengths, struggles, and inspirations—all intertwined in a continuous quest for reconciliation amid the tempest.

Yet Liora knew this exploration was only the beginning—a mere chapter in the saga that spanned centuries. The human experience remained far more intricate than the stories of gods and monsters. The divine whispers would continue to shape culture, motivating humanity to search for meaning, purpose, and healing amid the chaos. And in this pursuit, they would find glimpses of themselves intertwined with the celestial and monstrous alike—a harmonious tension that would echo through time.

The Blurred Lines of Myth and Reality

Ezekiel perched on the edge of a cloud, his wings folded neatly behind him, staring out over the sprawling landscape of humanity below. The Earth stretched before him like a tapestry woven with both brilliance and darkness, its hues shifting with the light of the sun and the shadows of its own despair. He had watched over this realm for centuries, guiding, protecting, and sometimes intervening. But today, as he surveyed the chaos that often seemed to define the human experience, he felt the burden of his role weigh heavily upon him.

In recent times, humanity's understanding of the celestial had become dangerously diluted, blurred by the mists of myth and legend. Once, tales of guardian angels inspired hope and faith. Now, they had become shadows of their former selves. Ezekiel remembered when children would whisper stories of luminous beings who swooped down to assist those in need. He longed for those innocent days when belief in angels flourished, unmarred by skepticism and the sharp edge of cynicism.

But there was a beauty in these myths, too. They were the echoes of a long-lost truth, shaped and reshaped by each generation's perception of the divine. As humans created stories, they filled the void where understanding should reside. They crafted gods and monsters, weaving threads of reality through the fabric of their narratives. Yet with every tale told, something sincere and unfiltered faded away. Ezekiel's heart ached with the realization that what once was a pure sense of awe had transformed into suspicion.

"I see you watching, Ezekiel." The voice was smooth as silk, laced with the intoxicating scent of temptation. Azazel appeared beside him with his signature devil-may-care charm, the darkness trailing behind him like a cloak.

Ezekiel's expression hardened. "You should not be here, Azazel. This isn't your realm."

"Ah, but I find it fascinating," Azazel replied, leaning casually against the celestial barrier that separated their domains. "The way they've crafted their narratives. When I roamed among them, they painted me as a monster, a demon of chaos. But does that not speak more to their fears than to my nature? They fashioned gods in their own image, reflecting their desires and nightmares."

Ezekiel turned his gaze back to the vibrant scene below, where humans scurried about their daily lives, weaving stories among themselves. "What is a god, if not the distilled essence of those they lead?" he mused aloud. "These beliefs shape destinies, mold societies, and define their morality. To guide a people is a heavy burden."

Azazel laughed, the sound echoing through the air like the soft crack of thunder. "You can feel that burden easily enough because you've striven to uphold the laws of heaven. I, however, embrace the chaos. My myth is a mess, yet it resonates with its raw truth. They understand me instinctively, giving me a strange kind of power over them."

"That power comes at a cost," Ezekiel countered. "Your chaos breeds despair. And that despair distances them from the divine."

"But at least they feel alive!" Azazel pressed, his eyes glimmering with mischief. "You watch over them with the rule of law, but they crave the fires of passion! They want freedom, and in their eyes, I grant that. They write tales of rebirth and loss, crafting an image of me that ignites their fervor while you remain boxed within the rigid confines of your heavenly narrative."

Ezekiel felt a stirring within him. How could he articulate the complexities of his existence to a being who had chosen to embrace the darker narrative?

"You think I don't understand their yearning for freedom? In every drop of ink that spills from a human heart, in every prayer sent skyward, they grapple with their existence and search for divine meaning. It does not diminish our purpose to offer solace, even within structure."

"Yes, but structure breeds complacency," Azazel shot back. "It creates mythologies that blind them to the beauty of uncertainty. Look at their art!" He gestured with a broad sweep of his hand toward an artist below, splashing colors onto a canvas as though trying to capture the very essence of life. "It is chaos that gives birth to creation! Without the tension, there can be no masterpiece."

Ezekiel's brow furrowed, torn between admiration for the artist's spirit and the stark truth of Azazel's words. Humanity's struggles often manifested into art, music, and literature—each expression a swimming pool of mixed emotions, both tender and tumultuous. Yet, being a guardian angel meant embracing order and balance, maintaining a fragile peace that often went unnoticed—a story overshadowed by louder voices.

"It's not chaos I stand for," Ezekiel replied finally. "Love, compassion, and the belief that individuals can strive for something greater. I exist to remind them of the light amid darkness. They have created a mythology around that very scaffolding, intertwining their hopes and fears into tales of salvation, of intervention. Who may rise without digging deep into their heart's truth?"

Azazel's expression shifted slightly. "Yet many choose to overlook the divine, do they not? They cast us aside once the trials of faith become too burdensome. They distance themselves from the messiness of existence, missing the raw beauty."

Ezekiel shook his head. It was true—many turned their backs on faith in moments of difficulty, pointing fingers at the heavens rather than seeking to understand the struggle within. "This journey they traverse is adorned with challenges meant to press them closer to understanding. They build their faith through myth, even if they cannot fully comprehend it."

"But aren't they constructing their own prison?" Azazel whispered, his voice edged with intrigue. "They imprison themselves with the very mythology they cling to. They forge a narrative where love is conditional, where belief remains tethered to fear."

Ezekiel's breath hitched. It was easy to see how narratives took root. Generations of belief separated by the passage of time twisted their interpretations, morphing angels into something monstrous, divine beings into forgotten myths. Well-meaning guardians were painted as beings of judgment, while fallen beings were often the protagonists in tales sparking rebellion.

In that moment, Ezekiel felt the echoes of countless souls brushing against him. Each one held a story of struggle, faith, hope, and despair. Were the myths shaping their destinies or binding them to the fates they were taught? What weight did these stories hold? He could feel the battle within them, the yearning for something greater, something true.

As Ezekiel searched for answers in the depths of humanity's creation, he remembered a story told to him in passing—a tale woven from the fabric of an ancient civilization. It spoke of a phoenix rising, reborn from ashes, the symbols of renewal etched upon the very souls of those who lived among those flames. He longed for such rebirth in his own realm, for both angels and humans to navigate the complexities of existence together, refashioning the myths that defined them.

"Even you, Azazel, possess an element of truth wrapped in your chaos," Ezekiel said slowly, weighing each word carefully. "But look how your chaos has pushed humanity into conflict. These narratives need balance."

"Balance?" Azazel scoffed, lacing his tone with genuine disbelief. "Balance implies acceptance of the static. My existence challenges the fabric! It allows the texture to fray just enough for them to recognize their deepest fears!"

"And those fears turn them away from the divine," Ezekiel replied earnestly. "They lose themselves within their own darkness."

Azazel's laughter rang through the air again, yet it held a note of reflection this time. "Perhaps your will to embrace the light could illuminate their path. But my sweet chaos reveals the truths they need to confront, truths you seek to veil."

Ezekiel placed his hands on his knees, contemplating the ephemeral nature of both their existences. "Amid the conflict, there remains a need for dialogue, Azazel. I see it in their eyes. When they endure and overcome, they craft new myths. They redefine their realities, allowing fragments of hope to penetrate the dark. They are hungry for connection and understanding. It does not end only with despair. My role may be a guiding light, but their journey toward faith combines both light and shadow."

"Then, guardian angel, let us not write their myths for them," Azazel spoke, his voice low and contemplative. "Let them rise from the ashes of their own making and discover the truth. Together, we can weave new narratives."

Ezekiel looked towards the horizon, where the sun dipped low, casting soft golden hues across the landscape. "Perhaps. But in the end, the narratives they create must stem from within if they are to thrive. They may embrace love or fear to create salvation or destruction. Whatever story they ultimately tell, they must pen it from the depths of their hearts."

The sky darkened, hinting at the blend of day and night, order and chaos—each influencing the other as they danced to an ancient rhythm. Ezekiel still felt a heaviness in his spirit, overshadowed by the uncertainty gripping humanity's heart. Yet amid this uncertainty, he also sensed a faint glimmer of hope, a flicker of belief trying to break free from haunting shadows.

As he watched the artist below brush colors across the canvas, his heart swelled with the understanding that every single stroke embodied a myth, each layer adding depth to the narrative. The blurred lines of myth and reality were not boundaries—they were instead new paths forged along the way.

This understanding was a divine gift, enabling him to see that the stories of angels and humans would continue evolving. New myths would arise, shaped by their collective struggles, and the tales of fallen angels would dance among them, informing yet never constraining the human experience.

Ezekiel's spirit lifted, and he found resolution within himself. He would continue to guide, to illuminate the path of faith. Through their moments of doubt, joy, and rebirth, humans would forge new tapestries of stories, crafting a legacy that intertwined their darkness and light, angel and demon, myth and reality. And within that intricate web, they could reshape their destinies.

"Let the myths invite the chaos," Ezekiel murmured, "and mourn the shadows they once feared. For within those stories lies not only their pain but also their triumph."

Azazel regarded him with a flicker of admiration. "Perhaps, dear Ezekiel, you are more akin to me than you realize."

"In our differences lies balance," he replied, "and in that balance, a glimpse of the divine."

As the night fell over the land, Ezekiel spread his wings, strengthened by the understanding that the blurred lines of myth and reality were not barriers, but bridges—connections allowing both angels and humans to traverse realms, each learning and evolving through the stories they told. Those narratives breathed the power to shape their destinies, beckoning them toward hope's vibrant embrace.

4

The Offspring of Legends

Demigods and Heroes

In the verdant valleys of ancient Greece, where the whispering winds carried tales of gods and heroes alike, a legend was born—a story of intertwined destinies that would resonate through the ages. Within the mortal realm, teeming with vibrant life, existed a delicate balance, a thin veil separating the celestial and the human. This intersection held the key to something extraordinary: the demigods, hybrids born of the divine and the earthly.

These beings, products of unions between angels—those embodiment's of celestial grace and power—and humans—creatures of flesh and ambition— embodied a compelling duality. They were neither fully of the heavens nor entirely rooted in the earth's soil; instead, they occupied a liminal space, an existence filled with longing and expectation. Each of them carried within their veins the blood of their angelic progenitors, mingled with the vivid passions of their human heritage. Thus, they became vessels of contradictions, caught in a perpetual struggle to reconcile the vastness of the divine with the limitations of humanity.

Among these remarkable beings was a young woman named Lysandra. With rippling hair like spun gold and eyes that shone as bright as the stars, she walked the earth as a flesh-and-blood testament to her lineage. Her father, a guardian angel banished for harboring forbidden feelings for a human woman, had imparted his essence to a gift that both elevated and isolated her. This duality enveloped her life with complexities; she bore the spark of divinity, yet was forever tethered to the mundane experiences of humanity.

Lysandra carried the ability to commune with the elements. On some days, her laughter stirred the leaves into a wild, jubilant dance, while on others, her tears could summon a tempest, darkening the skies to mirror her internal turmoil. The villagers revered her as a spectral being, yet her heart felt the ache of loneliness, its melancholic echo amplified by their awe. They placed upon her the mantle of their expectations and aspirations, just as they looked to the gods for favor, seeking blessings she often felt inadequate to provide.

In a world rife with conflict and myth, the stakes of her existence became painfully clear as the winds of change began to stir. Rumors of dark entities encroaching from the shadows of the realms beyond tangible reality seeped into the whispers of the night. Spurned by the heavens and twisted into grotesque mockeries of their former glory, Monsters sought dominion over Earth, fueled by insatiable lust for power and revenge against their celestial counterparts. As Lysandra contemplated her identity, she felt the weight of duty settle upon her shoulders—the burden of being a demigod intertwined with the call to protect her human counterpart.

In the heart of the bustling city of Athens, stories of gallant deeds had become the heartbeats of living memory. In taverns and marketplaces, legends were born alongside the flames of passion and sacrifice. Heroes like Theseus, who slayed the Minotaur, and Perseus, who claimed Medusa's head, became revered figures, transforming from mere mortals into symbols of courage and tenacity. Yet, unbeknownst to them, these tales, woven into the very fabric of their lives, were also indelibly influenced by their own conflicts and struggles.

Lysandra wandered the cobblestone streets, her senses attuned to the pulsing energies of the city around her. Each passerby lived a story unto themselves—artisans crafting masterpieces, children playing amidst laughter, and philosophers debating the cosmos. The mosaic of their existence reflected the intricate tapestry of human experience. But as she gazed into the eyes of her fellow Athenians, she felt an unyielding tension, a unifying thread binding their fates to hers—one that compelled her to choose.

What did it mean to be a hero? Did it require the strength of her angelic heritage, or could it be found in embracing her human vulnerabilities? Lysandra often questioned her place within this grand narrative. While the angels in heaven revered her, concerned for her safety amidst the impending conflict, her heart tugged in another direction. She sensed that the call for a champion did not lie solely among the ranks of divine beings. Hidden within her mortal brethren lay the potential for greatness unimagined, an opportunity waiting to be unlocked.

In the sanctum of her thoughts, she felt an unexpected companionship with her ancestors—the countless demigods who walked before her, each a testament to love and sacrifice. She thought of Heracles, the strongman whose legendary labors had shaped his destiny, straddling the line between mortal frailty and divine power. She pondered the destinies of others, such as Achilles, whose fight for glory was marred by the shadows of betrayal and grief. What had they felt? Had they grappled with the notion of their lineage, wanting to forge their own path while basking in the light of expectations?

These reflections of ancient heroes urged Lysandra to venture beyond the familiar confines of Athens, toward an uncharted destiny she believed awaited her. With each passing day, she nurtured a growing resolve to find her purpose—a calling that surged through her veins, as vibrant as the life coursing through the rivers of the land. She felt the weight of her heritage shifting; forging ahead could either affirm her existence as a mighty demigod or plunge her deeper into the abyss of uncertainty.

One dusky evening, as the sun dipped below the horizon, painting the sky in strokes of gold and crimson, she made her choice. Lysandra ventured into the depths of the Forest of Shadows, a realm whispered about among the people, steeped in legends of beasts and lost souls. Within its dark embrace lay the specter of her fears and a flicker of hope—an understanding that monsters had once been divine, just like her.

With every step, the air thickened with tension, and the soft rustle of leaves turned into a symphony of whispers. She was not alone; shadows danced at the edges of her vision, revealing the hulking figures that concealed their sorrow and vulnerability beneath layers of armor forged from pain. And it was among those shadows that she spotted him a figure lost to despair, illuminated by the wavering radiance of the moon.

"Who dares tread in the domain of the forsaken?" he boomed, his voice echoing through the clearing.

Lysandra took a steadying breath, feeling the pulse of her ancestry guiding her resolve. "I am Lysandra, daughter of the guardian, a demigod who seeks to understand the path between worlds."

"Demigod," he scoffed, stepping forward into the moonlight, revealing a visage unmistakably filled with anguish. Beneath the jagged scars and gaunt features, remnants of celestial beauty intermingled with the monstrous form he now bore. "You wear your lineage like a mask. It grants you no protection here. Haven't you heard? We are nothing but twisted remnants of a forgotten hierarchy."

"What you say may be true," she replied, courage bolstering her voice, "but our choices define us. Each action, be it heroic or monstrous, shapes our fates. We cannot let the burdens of our ancestry weigh us down for eternity."

As Lysandra spoke, the mysterious figure's stance softened, ambiguity flickering behind his piercing gaze. "You speak of choices, but you have not tasted despair. You have not known the depths of failure that rot your soul. I am Azaroth, a fallen guardian doomed to remain in this shadow of existence."

Lysandra's heart ached for Azaroth; she sensed the depths of his sorrow, the eternal longing for redemption. "What happened to you is not just your story; it's part of our shared legacy. We can pave new paths, rise from the ashes of our shortcomings—it's what demigods are meant to do."

"You think you can encompass us all? Are you prepared to fight the darkness and the demons lurking within?" The challenge ignited a spark of fierce determination within Lysandra. "What if I am?"

The fire of her resolve seeped into Azaroth; he watched her with newfound interest. "The darkness is insatiable. It feasts upon our regrets and desires. I have borne witness to the sorrow of countless souls, yet you stand unafraid before me. Are you willing to join the lost, even if it means facing your fears head-on?"

At that moment, Lysandra knew she was no longer an isolated entity, chosen by divinity, yet yearning for acceptance. She felt the ties of her heritage intertwined with all those who battled their demons, seeking grace in a world that often offered none. "I embrace my legacy!" she declared, echoing through the shadowed forest. "Together, we can reclaim our stories."

Their gazes locked, and for the first time, Azaroth blinked away the raw veneer of resentment that had harbored in his heart. Beneath the burden of darkness lay the spark of life waiting to ignite, waiting for a champion to advocate for them. In that instant, they were no longer defined solely by their lineage or failures; they became the catalyst for change, driven by newfound purpose and unity.

As dawn emerged over the horizon, casting warm brilliance across the land, Lysandra stirred—a demigod resolute in her commitment to forge her own identity. She understood that the path ahead would be fraught with external and internal trials. Yet, she no longer walked alone; with Azaroth beside her, they embarked on a journey to become the legends yet to be written—a hybrid union of strength, hope, and the unyielding spirit to rise above the tumult of existence.

As they traversed the depths of the world's uncertainties, Lysandra and Azaroth began the painstaking process of seeking those like them— dispossessed, neglected, yet brimming with potential. Their quest was not merely for power but an exploration of identity, an attempt to illuminate the darkest corners of existence and redefine the legacy of past demigods.

As tales of their adventures spread across the realm, they discovered that heroes were not only born but could also be made by embracing the complexities of their existence. Together, they would etch their story upon the canvas of time, revealing the sanctity of choice, the beauty of sacrifice, and the unwavering truth that what is born of love— human or divine—always rises from the ashes of despair. And so, Lysandra and Azaroth set forth: the next generation of demigods, caught between worlds yet propelled by a shared legacy destined to unfold.

The Impact on History

Across the annals of history, hidden beneath the surface of recorded events, lie the stories of beings who straddle the line between the divine and the mortal. These beings, the offspring of angels and humans, have enriched the tapestry of myth and shaped the course of civilizations, igniting revolutions and altering the fates of nations. Their legacies, often cloaked in the guise of legend, weave a narrative that tests the boundaries of belief, leaving indelible marks on the hearts and minds of humankind.

The tale begins in ancient Sumer, where civilization first took root in the cradle of Mesopotamia. The temples of this land rose tall and proud, dedicated to deities whose whims were believed to steer the fates of mortals. Here, the sun god Utu, whose radiance brought warmth and life, fell in love with a mortal priestess named Ninsun. Their union bore Gilgamesh, a demigod who would become a legendary figure destined for greatness. It is said that the very breath of the gods flowed through his veins, granting him strength beyond that of ordinary men.

As Gilgamesh ascended to the throne of Uruk, tales of his feats echoed throughout the region. With the heart of a lion and the wisdom of the divine, he embarked on a quest for immortality—a journey that would reveal the limits of both godhood and humanity. He battled the ferocious Humbaba and tamed the wild Bull of Heaven, creatures of chaos unleashed by Ishtar, the love goddess scorned by his refusal. In Gilgamesh's interactions with the divine and mortal realms, the narrative transcended mere myth; it demonstrated humanity's eternal longing for connection, understanding, and transcendence.

The epic of Gilgamesh serves not simply as a story of heroism; it illuminates the complexities of leadership and the burden of knowledge. Through his adventures, he learns that eternal life is not attainable, yet the legacy left behind— the cities built, the knowledge shared—grants a form of immortality. His tale inspired generations, emboldening leaders and warriors to carve their names into history. In this way, Gilgamesh's dual nature fueled societal evolution, encouraging humankind to aspire toward the divine while grappling with their own mortal limitations.

Fast forward to the grandiosity of Ancient Greece, where the demigods shaped the foundational myths of Western civilization. Perhaps none are more renowned than Hercules, the son of Zeus and the mortal Alcmena, whose strength was rivaled only by his determination. From an early age, Hercules proved to be a force of nature, yet his journey was riddled with the repercussions of celestial lineage. Driven into bouts of madness by Hera, his divine stepmother, he turned against that he held dear, illustrating the tumultuous nature of being caught between two worlds.

Hercules' Twelve Labors beckoned not just heroic feats but also a poignant reflection on the trials of existence. Each labor served as a metaphorical reflection of humanity's struggles—battling internal demons, facing insurmountable odds, and ultimately striving to rise above adversity. His tales became the lifeblood of Greek culture, inspiring art, theater, and philosophical thought. The Greeks derived moral teachings and ideals of stoicism from his exploits, emphasizing courage, endurance, and the importance of striving for virtue amidst chaos.

His legacy did not remain confined to myth. The ideals associated with Hercules echoed through the ages, serving as a model during moments of societal upheaval. Revolutionary leaders , such as Alexander the Great, identified with Hercules and sought to emulate his virtues, leading campaigns that forever changed the world landscape. In the eyes of many, Hercules became a personification of ambition and strength, enabling a new definition of leadership that transcended lineage, uniting both mortals and demigods in a common cause.

Centuries later, in the heart of the Roman Empire, the threads of divine lineage continued to interlace with human history. It was said that Aeneas, a Trojan hero believed to be the son of the goddess Venus, would shape Italy's destiny. His journey from the ruins of Troy to the promised land of Italy became a foundational myth for the Romans, establishing the very fabric of their identity. Aeneas's virtue, his adherence to fate and duty, captured the imaginations of those living in an era characterized by political machinations and moral ambiguity.

In what would later be dubbed the Aeneid, Virgil crafted a narrative that not only recounted Aeneas' journeys but also reflected the Roman ethos, encapsulating virtue, sacrifice, and piety. The fusion of divine favor and personal resolve provided an inspirational model for the Roman citizenry who navigated tumultuous political landscapes, reminding them of their shared destiny and collective responsibility to honor their forebears.

Aeneas' struggles resonated with the civilian populace, who often found their agency limited in the sway of powerful leaders. The blend of myth and reality declared that the greatness of Rome relied on the virtues embodied in their ancestors, igniting a call for unity during times of crisis. This narrative of divine purpose and human agency became a touchstone for many leaders across subsequent eras, reminding them of their roots while urging them to forge new paths toward greatness.

As the epochs turned, hybrid beings continued to play pivotal roles in shaping significant historical events. The Middle Ages heralded the emergence of various hero tales, wherein knights embarked on quests fueled by divine inspiration. Figures such as King Arthur, believed by some to be of divine lineage—his mother, Igraine, is thought to have a connection to fairies— emerged as champions of hope during the dark times of feudal struggle. The Arthurian legends illuminated ideals of chivalry, loyalty, and justice, crafting the narrative of a noble ruler destined to protect his realm despite overwhelming challenges.

The Knights of the Round Table served a dual purpose in the collective folklore—embodying ideals of courtly love and valor while confronting their human failings. The quest for the Holy Grail, steeped in themes of divine grace and salvation, became synonymous with the drive toward higher aspirations. The struggles Arthur and his knights faced mirrored those of everyday people, igniting a yearning for justice and community within a fractured society plagued by corruption.

The legacy of King Arthur and his brethren left an indelible mark on the cultural landscape, inspiring movements across centuries as they confronted tyranny and sought a just society. The ideals of Arthurian legend reverberated throughout the medieval courts and beyond, influencing various uprisings against oppression. Lancelot's love, Guinevere's betrayal, and the ultimate downfall of Camelot portrayed the fragility of both power and human relationships, allowing later generations to discern the moral complexities that govern human affairs.

Art and literature flourished under divine inspiration and creative genius as the Renaissance dawned. Here, allegories of demigods infused the era, manifesting through figures like Leonardo da Vinci, who, shrouded in divinity, sought to capture the essence of humanity amidst the backdrop of celestial inspiration. Da Vinci's relentless pursuit of knowledge and innovation reflected the lineage of heroes gone by, a continuation of the legacy embodied by the demigods of old who once walked the realms alongside mortals.

With every stroke of his brush, da Vinci awakened the spirit of curiosity that defined the Age of Enlightenment—a revolution not wrought by swords but by the pen and brush. His explorations in anatomy, engineering, and art challenged the perceived boundaries of reality, bringing forth a new understanding of the intersection between the divine and the mortal. Herein lies an invitation to all of humankind to strive for greatness, regardless of their lineage—a call echoed throughout time by every demigod who dared to dream.

However, the stories of these hybrid beings are not simply tales of heroism and valor; they remind us that greatness comes at a cost. Amid the flourishing art and revolutionary ideals, the specter of conflict loomed large, revealing the darker truths of ambition and power. Throughout history, hybrid beings have stoked fires of rivalry, their dual nature impelling them to forge alliances while simultaneously inciting discord.

The Reformation, for instance, saw figures like Martin Luther arise, echoing the calls of demigods past, challenging the very foundation of a power structure firmly rooted in the divine. The clash between Luther and the Catholic Church encapsulated the essence of a divine rebellion, as newly empowered voices sought to reshape society towards accountability and personal belief. Luther's legacy as a transformative figure forever altered the landscape of religion, empowering individuals to explore faith beyond institutional constraints. Yet, the friction resulting from his rebellion stoked intolerance that led to wars and bloody confrontations.

In these moments of profound transformation, one can see how demigods serve as catalysts, reflecting humanity's strengths and vulnerabilities. They embody that innate drive propelling humanity toward progress while serving as cautionary tales of ambition gone awry.

The American Revolution emerged as another significant testament to the impact of hybrid beings on human history. Figures like Thomas Jefferson and Benjamin Franklin, inspired not only by the enlightenment ideals of democracy but also by the notion of divine right, sought to forge a new path. The revolutionary spirit ignited through the writings of these leaders found its roots in the belief that all individuals, much like the demigods of yore, could rise to greatness through the virtue of their actions.

Jefferson's Declaration of Independence resonated with the cries of new generations yearning for freedom, as they tore down the vestiges of colonial oppression. Here, the legacy of heroes past proved essential to mobilizing the masses, reflecting the intertwined narrative of demigods influencing history. Yet, the revolution ultimately revealed the fragility of human ambition—a dichotomy of liberty and slavery that would sow the seeds of further conflict down the line.

The tumult of the 20th century laid bare the profound impact of hybrid beings on history, most notably during the world wars. Figures like Winston Churchill, who embodied determination and courage, emerged as modern-day demigods, rallying nations in adversity. Churchill's oratory became the lifeline of a faltering nation, calling forth valor amidst the chaos of war. His lineage as a leader steeped in remarkable heritage imbued him with the capital of legacy, allowing him to inspire fervently.

Wherever the fabric of history unfolds, the echoes of these hybrid beings resonate. They redefine the narrative of human endeavor—the yearning for greatness interspersed with the burden of legacy. Their stories remain deeply woven into the collective consciousness, driving forward the very struggles that define us even today.

In our modern age, as humanity grapples with issues of identity, belonging, and purpose, the legacy of these demigods urges us to confront our complexities. The stories of past heroes ignite the flame of aspiration, reminding us that greatness can emerge from the most unlikely of circumstances. Much like the offspring of legends, each individual harbors the potential to leave a lasting impact on the world—a legacy shaped by choices, resilience, and the courage to confront the duality of existence.

As we contemplate the trajectory of history, the lessons imparted by these demigods reveal the fundamental truth that threads through the chaos of time; the intersection of myth and reality remains an enduring testament to the power of belief. The choices of our ancestors resonate within us, challenging us to embrace our own narratives, empowering us to reshape our destinies as we endeavor to emulate the courageous legacies left behind.

Through every triumph and catastrophe, the offspring of legends remind us that while they may exist beyond our reach, their influence forever inspires us to become the heroes of our own stories.

The Struggle for Acceptance

The night sky was a tapestry of stars, each flickering light a distant reminder of the celestial realms above. Yet, beneath the brilliance of the cosmos, the earth felt heavy, charged with whispers of judgment and uncertainty. Rhea stood at the edge of the hillock, a demigod caught in the twilight of her identity, her heart beating like a drum echoing through the silence of the night.

Her mortal mother had passed down stories of the gods, beautiful, untouchable beings who wove the fabric of existence with their ethereal hands. Her father, an angelic warrior of light, was a figure woven into legend—seraphic and distant, a symbol of beauty and grace. Yet, Rhea felt the distance all too well, for her very existence bridged the gap between those two worlds, and in doing so, she had become a target for prejudice and misunderstanding.

"Rhea!" a voice called from the shadows, pulling her from her reverie. It was Callen, her closest friend and confidant. He approached with caution, the glow of the moon catching the sharp angles of his youthful face. He knew her struggles, yet there was always a flicker of hope in his eyes , making her heart swell with gratitude.

"Are you alright?" he asked, concern lacing his tone.

"I'm weary, Callen. Every day feels like I'm walking on a tightrope, trying to balance so many expectations," she confessed, turning her gaze to the horizon where the last remnants of the sun faded into darkness.

Callen stepped beside her, their shoulders almost touching. "You're more than what others see. You blend both realms, and that's a gift, not a curse."

"But what if they don't see it that way?" Rhea's voice trembled, thick with emotion. "What if they only see the monster in me?"

"That's their struggle, not yours," he replied firmly, but Rhea could see the hint of doubt in his eyes. Callen always tried to reassure her, yet they both knew the harsh realities that came with her lineage.

As a demigod, Rhea was caught between two worlds—neither fully human nor entirely angelic. The mortals treated her with suspicion, whispering tales of her monstrous heritage, while the angels saw her as a reminder of the fallen. Her heart mirrored the world above, fractured and searching for solace.

Focusing her gaze on the valley below, she saw figures moving in the moonlight—fellow villagers preparing for a celebration of harvest. Laughter floated on the breeze, but it felt like a distant echo. They would welcome everyone, yet when it came to her, they would turn away, their smiles fading into polite masks.

"Perhaps I could leave," Rhea mused aloud, surprising even her. "Maybe if I remove myself from their lives, I could find peace."

Callen's eyes widened in protest. "You can't just run away, Rhea! You belong here, with us."

"Do I?" she replied, her voice steely. "Belonging is a two-way street, Callen. If they cannot accept me, how can I claim this place as my home?"

A silence stretched between them, the weight of truth hanging heavily in the air. Callen bit his lip, his brows furrowing in thought. "We can change their perceptions. If they see how brave you are, how you've fought to protect this village from the monsters that lurk in the shadows, they'll..."

"They'll still see me as one of them," Rhea interrupted, her frustration boiling . "I saved them from those beasts only to be reminded that I look like what they fear. I can hear them when they talk behind my back. They think I am one step away from becoming them. A monster."

The words fell between them like ash, heavy and suffocating, casting a shadow over their shared moment. Callen searched her face, and before he could speak, she turned her back on the valley, feeling the sting of tears at the edges of her vision.

"Let's go back to the village," he suggested softly, trying to bridge the distance that had grown between them.

"Why? So they can celebrate without me? I won't be a prisoner in their farce."

Rhea felt the anger rise in her chest, and for a moment, she longed to unleash it, to let the power coursing through her veins break free. The essence of the divine thrummed within her, a reminder of her father, of the beauty and the chaos she carried.

In her heart, she knew Callen was right—she had fought for her place among humans, battling their fears and the monsters that threatened to consume them. But each time she stepped into the light, she felt the weight of their judgment pressing down on her, and in the darkness, she feared she might one day become what she was fighting against.

"Please, Rhea," Callen's voice cut through her turbulent thoughts, soft but unwavering. "You have to know that not everyone feels that way. You have allies. Just look at me."

His earnestness melted her defenses slightly. They had been friends since childhood, and she could not bear to push him away, no matter how heavy her heart felt.

"Alright," she relented, letting out a shaky breath. "I'll try."

The night wrapped around them as they descended the hill, the air cold and laced with the scent of earth and decaying leaves. The sounds of the harvest celebration grew louder, and an unsettling mix of hope and dread twisted in her stomach.

As they entered the village square, colorful lanterns illuminated the faces of the villagers. Joyful laughter echoed around her, blending with the music that played at the heart of the gathering. Yet Rhea felt like an outsider in her own skin, her legs heavy as she tentatively stepped forward.

"Look, it's Rhea!" a voice chimed, and the crowd shifted easily. For a heartbeat, they turned toward her, expressions mingled with curiosity and wariness. It felt like a spell-shattering, fracturing the flicker of joy in the air.

"Let's see if she brought her monster friends," another voice cut through the air, laced with mockery. Laughter followed, and Rhea felt like she had been ripped from the warmth of belonging, thrown into the cold waters of judgment.

She clenched her fists at her sides, recalling her father's teachings on grace and power. "I may be one of them," she thought, "but I am not to be a monster."

Yet their disdain pooled around her, suffocating and relentless. Her heart pounded, the internal battle raging—the urge to flee versus the desire to stand her ground. Callen glanced back at her, his expression pleading, wanting her to say the words that could turn the tide.

"Let's dance!" He suddenly shouted, attempting to rally the crowd back into a celebration. In his voice, she heard an echo of what she yearned for most—a sense of community, acceptance, and understanding.

As the villagers gradually shifted their attention to the festivities, Rhea took a breath, steeling herself. The music called to her, a gentle whisper inviting her to join in. So, she let the melody wash over her, stepping forward slowly, feeling the weight of unkind eyes.

But as she moved closer to the center, her mother's smiling face flashed in her thoughts, and for a moment, Rhea felt buoyed by that enduring love. She wanted to dance and celebrate what she had—her unique identity, strengths, and lineage. She could not let fear define her.

She began to move, then suddenly, she was twirling, free from the confines of others' judgments. The music flowed through her in waves, each note igniting the spark within. Laughter bubbled from her lips like a long-suppressed joy.

"Come on, Rhea!" Callen laughed, joining her, and before long, a few villagers hesitantly stepped closer. The beat of the drums urged them forward. "See? You're infectious!"

Laughter erupted between them, and despite the cloudy beginnings of the evening, warmth began to fester in Rhea's chest. For a moment, she forgot the cruelty that lay outside, lost in the dance , rhythm, and celebration's essence.

But as she moved, the shouts began again. "Watch out! She's going to summon a horde!"

The laughter morphed into uncomfortable chuckles, and Rhea faltered, her heart hardening again. "It's never enough. They never see beyond their fears," she thought darkly.

Then a weighty silence fell over the gathered crowd, and she turned to the source of the disruption. A figure stood at the edge of their celebration, draped in shadows, a sight that sent shivers down Rhea's spine. The air around him hummed with an unsettling energy , making her instincts flare.

Azrael, a known enforcer of the boundaries between realms, stood watching her with eyes like smoldering coals. The crowd tensed, the laughter dissipating as fear coiled around them.

"Why do you celebrate with a monster, dear villagers?" Azrael called out, his voice smooth like silk but edged with steel. "Do you not fear the blood that runs through her veins? Will you be the next victim of her chaos?"

Gasps echoed through the square as Rhea felt the stabs of anger and humiliation boiling inside her. The villagers recoiled at the very thought, revealing the raw nerves of prejudice that clung to their hearts.

She took a step forward, ready to confront the looming darkness threatening to overshadow their fragile gathering. "I am not your enemy!" she shouted, her voice echoing with conviction. "I am here to protect you from the true monsters that linger in the shadows."

A murmur rippled through the crowd, some faces showing hesitation, others pure fear. Callen stepped by her side, his hand resting reassuringly on her shoulder. "You know the truth, Rhea. You can convince them."

But Azrael's laughter cut through the tension like a knife. "And if she fails? Will you endanger yourselves for the sake of a failure?" His words dripped with venom, each syllable carefully chosen to incite fear.

Rhea's heart sank as she scanned the conflicted faces before her. "Am I a failure? Is my existence a curse?" Doubt crept into the back of her mind, but she fought against it, channeling her spirit into clarity and strength.

"What do you fear? The power of my heritage or the might of my heart?"

she shouted, letting the determination spill from her lips.

Others shifted closer, caught in the flames of her passion. "She fought for us! She protected us!" someone chimed in from the crowd.

"Yes!" another voice joined, emboldened.

A s they contemplated her words, a swelling sense of unity began to unfurl among the villagers. Azrael's smile flickered, and for a brief moment, Rhea felt the tides shifting.

"Your false hope will only lead to devastation," Azrael warned, but Rhea stood firm, refusing to let fear dominate any longer.

"I choose to embrace my heritage!" she proclaimed, her voice steady and unwavering. "I may be a child of the fallen, but it does not define my heart. I will prove that monsters are not born; they are made by fear and misunderstanding!"

The village erupted, voices overlapping, fear wrestling with hope that had been long buried. As her heart thundered in her chest, she caught Callen's gaze, pride sparkling in his eyes.

In that moment, the veil of doubt began to lift. Rhea felt their acceptance start to bloom, fragile yet vibrant. The shadows receded, allowing light to bathe the gathering once more.

With renewed determination, she stepped forward, her posture unyielding as her heart whispered of acceptance. "Let me show you the truth of both worlds within me."

As Rhea reached toward the villagers, each sharing glimmers of understanding, she realized the true battle she faced was not the monsters lurking in the night, but rather the journey of acceptance and the courage to embrace every part of her being.

And as she took that plunge, she embraced her identity—the daughter of light and shadows—demigod, protector, and a warrior of the heart. The whispers of doubt were drowned out by the symphony of unity, reverberating through the night and forging a connection she yearned for all along.

The struggle for acceptance would carry on, but in that climactic moment, Rhea became the bridge between realms—embracing both light and dark, refusing to be defined solely by the past, ready to bear the weight of her legacy as she stepped into her future.

5

The Battle for Earth

The Clashing Realms

The sky was an otherworldly canvas of roiling clouds swirling with hues of crimson and indigo. The air crackled with energy, tangible and alive, a precursor to the cataclysmic events unfolding below. Earth, a fragile speck caught in the middle of cosmic warfare, became the stage for the ultimate clash as angels and monsters spilled into the human realm, their ancient grievances materializing in a clash that threatened to obliterate everything in its wake.

A sudden gust swept through the abandoned city, rattling the skeletal remains of storefronts and shattered glass. Buildings that once flourished with human life now stood as crumbling relics of a forgotten era, a battleground nestled in the heart of chaos. Somewhere above, unseen yet omnipresent, the celestial war commenced, casting its shadows upon the still-hidden lives of mortals.

Ezekiel soared through the storm-tossed sky, his wings unfurling to catch the fierce winds. A guardian angel by nature, his heart was heavy with the weight of divine responsibility. Today, he bore the burden of fierce conviction like never before. Below him, the skyline flickered like dying embers as flashes of light illuminated pockets of darkness, revealing a scene of unimaginable destruction.

An army of fallen angels, led by Azazel, swept down from their fallen realms, their grotesque forms twisting the very fabric of reality. Ezekiel's heart pounded. He remembered his own battles, the choices he'd made, and the consequences that lingered like ghosts. His eyes narrowed as he caught sight of Seraphiel, a fellow seraph, grappling with his own demons as he faced the oncoming tide of chaos.

"Ezekiel!" Seraphiel's voice pierced through the maelstrom, filled with urgency. "We must protect them! The humans—this world!" His wings flared, shimmering with a radiant glow that cut through the gathering darkness. Every beat of their wings seemed to scorn the encroaching shadows, but deep within, uncertainty gnawed at Seraphiel. Was this battle—this sacrifice—worth the lives of so many?

Ezekiel landed near him, his heart racing in tandem with the pulsing energy surrounding them. "We can't let them suffer," he replied, fists clenched at his sides. "Not again." The memories of previous wars haunted him, the lives lost, the devastation wrought by the battles among their kind.

A clang of metal twisted him back to the present. Monsters darted between the ruined buildings, their laughter echoing with dark mirth. Teeth glinted, sharp, and predatory. They had come to reclaim what they believed was rightfully theirs. And yet, even amid the chaos, the undercurrent of deception ran deep.

The city's long-abandoned streets transformed into a macabre theater of war. Angel and monster clashed, divinity meeting chaos in a violent ballet. The ground shook as a hulking figure—once an angel of light—now a twisted reflection of his former self—spelled doom with every movement. Azazel's army was relentless, emboldened by the desperation of those who once basked in the glow of grace.

Ezekiel found himself on the precipice of battle, eyes scanning the horizon where ethereal light met sinister shadows. Yet, in this moment of chaos, he felt a flicker of something more profound—a connection with humanity. The mortals fled from their homes, panic-stricken and confused. They were caught in the crossfire of a cosmic dispute, and the angels' commitment to their protection ignited a fire within Ezekiel's core.

"Get them to safety!" he shouted to Seraphiel, who nodded with determination etched on his face. "We can't allow these beasts to touch them. I'll draw their attention. You protect the innocents!"

Ezekiel took to the skies with a mighty thrust, his wings sparkling with divine light—a beacon urging mortals to move. He could see the fear among humans mirrored in their eyes as they looked up, not knowing who to trust. A monstrous shadow swept from the side, a beastly form lurching toward a family caught in the open.

"NO!" Ezekiel roared, adrenaline surging through him as he dove downwards. His hand ignited with fervor, a brilliant light cascading like a waterfall as he barreled into the oncoming shadow.

The collision sent shock waves through the air, blinding brilliance illuminating the space between angel and monster. Ezekiel felt the impact vibrate through his body, and despite the terror locked behind hollow eyes, he could not help but feel pity for those once so pure. In desperation, Azazel's followers were willing to serve a master whose allure brought chaos.

"Fools!" Azazel's voice thundered from above, ringing with malevolence. His figure, a seraph tinged with darkness, hovered above the battlefield, eyes gleaming as he reveled in chaos. "You think you can save them? They shall be fodder for the darkness! Your efforts are meaningless!"

Ezekiel's heart sank, recognizing Azazel's taunts merely as false idols of power. Yet, somewhere within him, doubt bubbled up, whispering questions of whether they would truly succeed in protecting a realm indifferent to the celestial wars above. This was not just an attack on the people; it was an assault against hope itself.

A screech erupted nearby—another clash as Seraphiel engaged with a group of twisted demons painted with shades of despair and longing. His heart ached as he unleashed the fiery wrath of the heavens, yet something stirred within him. With every swing of his blade, he glimpsed the remnants of what he had abandoned. Was the angelic legacy—his legacy—worth spilling innocent blood?

"Seraphiel!" Ezekiel shouted amid the clamor, noting his friend's momentary hesitation against an opponent he had once called brethren. "Stand firm! They're grasping at shadows. Do not let their persuasion sway you!"

In that instant, Seraphiel forced himself to see beyond the monster, recognizing not just the grotesque form but the haunting, lost flicker beneath. These beings were his kin, once radiant like the stars; now, they were darkly disfigured reflections battling against fate.

Driven by this revelation, Seraphiel fought with renewed vigor, channeling his grief into courage as he stared down the dark figure before him—a fallen angel who had once served beside him.

"You were once one of us!" Seraphiel pleaded, voice steady amidst the chaos. "You don't have to do this. We can mend what was broken!"

The fallen angel hesitated, caught in the dichotomy of memory and malevolence. In that instant of uncertainty, another monster surged forward, knocking the fallen angel aside and thrusting Seraphiel into a strategic bind.

"Time to choose, brethren!" Azazel's cackle echoed from the towers above, laughter mingling with the awful sounds of battle. "Either embrace your fate as I have or relinquish your power! Surrender to this world's impending doom!"

Seraphiel felt the darkness close around him, seeking to suffocate the last remnants of hope. Beside him, Ezekiel fought valiantly against the torrent of monsters, his wings cutting through the air as he battled against betrayal and self-doubt.

More beings surged forward, the darkened army advancing with relentless force, drawing on raw instinct rather than strategic tactics. Chaos danced around them as the ground buckled under the weight of their battle, with the earth itself seeming to scream in protest.

"Seraphiel!" Ezekiel shouted once again, desperation lacing his voice. "We cannot waver. They will crush us if we lose sight of our purpose!"

But even as they fought, even amid the violence, clarity rose above confusion. Seraphiel steadied his breath, forging ahead and resolving that the power of compassion—of light—was worth fighting for. He renewed his determination, channeling memories of camaraderie, unity, and the ancient bonds shared with his fallen brethren.

He dove back into the fray with renewed vigor, carving paths through the shadows, lighting an ethereal fire that tore through the darkness. Ezekiel could see it—his brethren taking a stand, defying Azazel's hold, and in that defiance, hope blossomed anew.

United in their struggle, the seraphim pressed on, rallying the remnants of intention within their fallen brethren. They fought not just for humanity but to reclaim their own light to honor the celestial bond that tied all beings together.

Yet as they forged ahead, the tumult of battle surged, shifting alliances in the blink of an eye. A monster charged straight toward Seraphiel, a maw filled with rage. He prepared to strike, but for a fleeting moment, he sensed—no, felt—an echo of regret. In that split second, his resolve faltered.

"Stay strong!" Ezekiel called, intercepting the beast mid-flight. "You cannot afford to falter now!"

Their combined light illuminated the battlefield momentarily, but the darkness receded only to grow ever more relentless. Azazel watched, eyes narrowed with sinister amusement as Seraphiel's internal conflict played out before him. The fallen had found their nucleus of light only to be challenged by their own darkness.

"Join me, Seraphiel!" Azazel beckoned, his voice a velvet snare. "Why struggle against the inevitable? Embrace the chaos—I can offer you power, all that you desire!"

Seraphiel felt a powerful tug, his history entwined with Azazel's dark promises. An endless abyss lay before him—flashes of power, prestige, and absolute dominion. Yet buried deep within him lingered indelible memories— of laughter, camaraderie, and a purpose far greater than power alone.

Bolstered by those memories, he steadied himself, shoulders squared against the formidable foe. "I will stand for the light! Even if I fall, I will not succumb to your darkness!"

Blasting forward, Seraphiel summoned the full power of his light, pushing against the shadows. The very fabric of the ground shuddered beneath them, and in that moment, the true stakes unveiled themselves. This was a clash not merely for individual factions but for the very soul of creation itself.

In another breath, the sky erupted. Stars shimmered behind a curtain of darkness, casting chaotic patterns across the field of battle. Monsters shrieked and roared, their cries echoing among the ruins, yet from them emerged a recognizable hue—the fabric of light birthed through anger, hope, and defiance.

Suddenly, as though time itself froze, Seraphiel noticed the movement of shadows bending—two monsters shifting sides to join the angels, lingering doubts giving way to a desperate desire for redemption. Their hearts pulsed with what remained of their humanity.

"This is our moment!" Ezekiel cried, his wings unfurling above the culmination of chaos. "Together, we can shatter this darkness!"

And with that powerful declaration—the celestial blend of seraphim and fallen angels erupted forth, converging upon the dark forces like a storm. The tide of battle began to shift. It was a frenzied interplay of light and shadow, grace and despair, as both sides were forced to reassess their motivations.

Azazel howled in rage, realizing he was losing his grip, charging forward in a last-ditch effort to reclaim the power he so desperately coveted. The ground quaked beneath his fury, his form twisting into that of nightmares—twice the height and thrice the strength, a true monstrosity.

"Fools! Do you think you can stand against me? Your light is fading!" he bellowed, venom lacing every syllable.

Yet, with newfound resolve, Seraphiel and Ezekiel pressed on. The bond that had once defined their choices fueled their journey; they fought for themselves and the chance to mend the rift between realms.

This battle, their struggle—an intricate tapestry woven from centuries of conflict—spoke with a sound deeper than mere clashing steel or shrieks of agony. It whispered of hope, growth, and the power of unity against the threat of despair.

As the fog of battle thickened, it became clearer that alliances—once deemed impossible—were being forged right in the heart of chaos. For every monster that tore at the heavens, another seraph rose to the challenge, convinced that righteousness could conquer even the deepest of the abyss.

The stakes soared higher, each decision rippling through the realms as the cosmic balance slowly began to shift. In the heart of the storm, the angels and their former brethren became reflections of one another—a haunting reminder that even in darkness, light had its place.

As light seeped through the cracks of despair, hearts filled with purpose surged forward. Every choice led them closer to the climax, where the fabric of existence would either bind together or unravel forever.

Ezekiel and Seraphiel, against all odds, found their courage amidst the raging storm. With every swing and radiant blast of light, they challenged Azazel's reign—seeking to reclaim not just their realms, but the essence of what it meant to be divine, to be truly free.

And as they confronted their past, they gathered strength not only from themselves but buoyed by the knowledge that salvation might lie in their own struggles and their willingness to embrace vulnerability amidst the tumult of war.

The clash of realms had begun in earnest, the battle far from over, yet hope started to take root in the most unlikely of places. Human lives intertwined with celestial causes, and as they fought the encroaching oblivion, the dawn of unity broke on the horizon—a possibility still flickering despite the monstrous shadows.

Together, they surged forward into the heart of battle, where the echoes of their ancestors would guide their way, undeterred by recklessness or despair. With light around them, they would carve a path through darkness, hand in hand, battling for the very soul of what it meant to be alive.

Humanity's Role

The sky was a grim slate, suffused with a dark haze that clung to the horizon. Silent screams echoed in the air, whispers of fear and determination weaving through the throngs of humanity gathered in the town square. What once was a bustling center of life and community lay now in ruins, the remnants of shattered glass and debris a stark reminder of the once-vibrant world. In this crucible of destruction, ordinary people would soon have to awaken the extraordinary within themselves.

Liora stood amidst the crowd, her heart racing like the drumbeats of war that thrummed beneath the surface of the chaos. She had never considered herself a hero. Her life had revolved around the simple joys of art and family, the beauty in everyday moments. Yet here, at the precipice of darkness, she felt a calling that resonated deep within her soul. With each passing moment, she could sense the mounting tide of despair, a weight that threatened to engulf everyone around her. But beneath that weight, something else stirred—the flickering light of hope.

A shiver coursed through Liora's spine, not from cold but from the urgency of her visions, visions that had come to her in fragments. Images of angels clashing with monsters, the skies ablaze with the fury of celestial battle, and herself standing firm between the two. The burden of those sights pressed heavily on her. She had to act—not just for her sake, but for the sake of everyone around her.

"Listen!" she called out, her voice a beacon rising above the cacophony. There was no grand eloquence to her words, just raw sincerity. "We can't let fear control us. We've witnessed the darkness, but we have a light within us, too. We have to stand together!"

Her words seemed to momentarily suspend the chaos around her. Those in the crowd began to turn their eyes toward her, drawn by the earnestness in her voice. From a sea of faces etched with uncertainty, one by one, they began to step forward, emboldened by the quiet spark of defiance igniting within them.

As Liora glanced over her shoulder, she saw Ezekiel, the guardian angel who had watched over her until now, hovering just out of reach. His presence was both a comfort and a challenge—a reminder of the celestial war engulfing their world, a stark contrast to the humanity that thrived in their fragile bond.

"I can't protect you forever, Liora," he said, his voice low and grave as he approached. "You must find your strength and rally those around you. The time for hiding is over."

"Yes," Liora replied, feeling the weight of his expectation and belief. "But I can't do it alone. I've seen how the darkness affects people—their fears, their desperation. Together, we can fight back."

"I will stand with you," Ezekiel promised, the certainty in his voice adding to her resolve. "But you must bring them together. Their hearts must align, for this war is more than blades and visions; it's a battle of spirits."

With Ezekiel's words heralding her purpose, Liora turned back to the crowd, emboldened anew. "You all know the stories—the tales of heroes from ages past. But this is our time. You, each of you, can be a hero. It's not about strength or weapons; it's about courage, hope, and the bonds we share."

A murmur rippled through the crowd, acknowledgment flickering in their eyes. Liora's heart swelled; she could feel their determination coalescing into something palpable, something that hummed with purpose. She could see Lee—a humble carpenter—stepping forward, his hands calloused but sturdy. Behind him, the librarian, Ms. Hargrove, who had spent her life igniting the love of stories in the young, stood firm, the weight of her years now transformed into a steely conviction.

Others joined, too: the baker, the shopkeeper, the teacher, people who had lived ordinary lives, now all pulled into extraordinary circumstances. As they stood shoulder to shoulder, Liora caught sight of a child, no more than ten years old, clutching a wooden sword he had made himself. His innocence tugged at her heartstrings. "If a child can dream of being a hero, then surely adults can stand and fight!"

"Aye!" shouted Lee, raising his fist. The fire in his belly ignited a wave of affirmation that swept through the crowd. "Aye, we'll fight!"

As voices rallied, a sense of unity bolstered them. Liora could see that they were no longer just survivors; they were warriors in their own right. Yet, she also sensed the fear lurking just beneath the surface. They were not combatants, nor were they experienced in the ways of war. Another voice rose, trembling but resolute. It was Janice, a nurse who had tended to the wounded from past skirmishes. "We may not have swords or shields, but we have courage and care for one another. That makes us stronger than any weapon!"

Liora beamed with pride, gratitude flooding her heart for the bond that had formed. At that moment, she understood that they were creating a coalition of fighters and a family united against the encroaching darkness.

But as her purpose solidified, doubt began to creep in—was this enough? Would sheer courage and desire be sufficient to hold off the chaos that churned just out of sight? A disquieting thought surfaced: what if they were simply offering themselves as sacrifices to the monstrous tide that threatened to consume them all?

"I can't promise that we won't face pain," Liora spoke, her voice cutting through her thoughts. "Some of us may not return. But if we don't stand together now, then we'll surely perish alone."

"Then let us face this battle together!" shouted Lee, his voice rallied by every soul that stood beside him. "Let them know that we—ordinary people— will not bow to monsters."

The resolve of the crowd deepened, and Liora felt a shift in the atmosphere. She closed her eyes for a moment, breathing deeply to capture the energy swimming around her. In that fleeting silence, she summoned the vision of the world she had seen—the stark contrast of darkness and the fragile glow of hope. They could be the lantern on this dark night.

"Then we march!" she declared, thrusting her hand into the air as if summoning the strength of a thousand battles. "We gather our sorrows and empower our spirits. We channel our love for one another into a force that can drive back any darkness!"

The crowd erupted in cheers, a wave of determination crashing through them as they rallied around Liora. They moved as one, bound by a shared purpose, gathering makeshift weapons—wooden staffs, kitchen knives, anything that could offer them even the smallest measure of defense.

As they prepared to march towards the heart of the chaos, Liora's thoughts wandered to the stories that had inspired her, tales of those who had faced insurmountable odds. In each story, triumph followed sacrifice. But these were not just stories now; they were the fabric of their reality, woven intricately into their beings.

Setting out, they focused on the path ahead. The air was thick with uncertainty, yet Liora could sense the spirits of her companions rising with each step.

As they drew nearer to the outskirts of what had once been a peaceful neighborhood, the tangible remnants of their lives lay scattered amongst the rubble. A child's broken toy here, a crumbling wall covered with faded paint that once told stories of joy—all memories now sullied by the shadow of monsters lurking just beyond their perception.

Suddenly, Liora's heart quickened. In the distance, she could hear the sour echo of laughter, a dark and malevolent sound that sent chills racing down her spine. The monstrous entities that had plagued them were drawing closer, the air thick with an intensity that prickled her skin.

"Stay tight!" Liora called, instinctively moving to position herself at the front. "Do not let fear break our line."

But as they pressed forward, a figure materialized before them at the edge of a crumbling wall. A hulking shape with grotesque features that seemed to shift in the dim light. It let out a deafening roar, sending tremors through the ground. It was a monster born of darkness and despair, one that embodied their deepest fears.

The crowd recoiled instinctively, but Liora felt the courage swell within her like a rising tide. The time for fear was over. The townspeople could not go back now; to retreat would mean surrender.

"Together," Liora urged her voice a fierce whisper now sharp with urgency. "Stand together!"

With that simple command igniting the spark within them, Liora took a daring step forward, eyes locked onto the beast that towered before them. In her heart, she could feel the warmth of her companions bolstering her; she was not alone in this fight. Each heartbeat echoed with purpose, a reminder that they were more than just bodies against a beast—they were a manifestation of hope.

"Fight!" She screamed, thrusting her wooden staff forward, which she had picked up along their way. A river of courage surged through her veins as she felt the energy of those around her respond.

The townspeople surged forward, moving in unison, bolstered by adrenaline and the sheer force of their shared resolve. Even as fear cloaked them like a shroud, empowerment sparked between their frantic breaths. As they pressed forward, Liora could see them transforming into an unbreakable line.

They met the monster's roar with their own shouts of defiance, keeping their spirits high as they fought against the chaos. Each strike they made, every scream they let loose, carried the weight of their humanity—a testament to their resilience against a force greater than themselves.

"Forward! Push!" shouted Lee, rallying their collective strength.

Liora fought alongside them, her own heart racing with a blend of fear and exhilaration. In the muddied soil, hope began to take root as they focused on defending one another. They were drawing upon the very essence of community—compassion, support, and fierce determination.

But as fierce as their hearts burned, the creature instinctively swiped through the crowd, causing chaos to erupt within moments. A deafening crash silenced their shouts as it knocked several people off their feet.

"Stay united!" Liora yelled, her voice trying to cut through the despair. The cries of her fellow warriors filled her ears, but she hardened her resolve. Every face she saw—stricken by fear yet striving for hope—instilled within her the need to fight back.

Ezekiel soared overhead, shimmering with celestial light as he swooped down at the beast, his sword gleaming with divine power. For a moment, Liora caught a glimpse of the true battle unfolding in the heavens above, where angels fought against the darkness that threatened their world.

"This is not just a fight for survival—it's a fight for our very existence!" he roared, delivering blows filled with the weight of justice. Each clash resonated through the battlefield, a divine melody amidst primal chaos.

Using this surge of energy bestowed upon her, Liora plunged deeper into her own gifts, feeling the connections she held with those around her. The depth of human emotion, especially love and courage, combined with divine intervention, created a vortex of power that was almost tangible.

"Together!" Liora rallied once more as she felt the urgency swell within her. They lifted their makeshift weapons high, uniting as a singular entity, embodying every whisper shared in despair and every tender touch amidst the ruins of their past.

As if acknowledging their courage, the monster hesitated, confusion flickering in its twisted visage. The darkness had underestimated the light within them. They were not simply combatants; they were beings fueled by dreams of a world free from fear, and they had rallied together for a cause greater than themselves.

With one final roar, the collective energy of humanity surged forth. They charged their fear, their strength, and their hope into one valiant surge, thrusting toward the enemy, aligning their hearts in unity.

"Now!" Liora shouted, guiding the momentum of their fight. The wave of humanity hit the monstrous beast like a thunderous crash, a deluge of resolve washing over them.

The ground shook beneath them, the clash of wills echoing through the very fabric of reality. In that moment, it became starkly clear to Liora that this was not merely a battle against monsters but a pivotal moment heralding the courage found in communal strength bolstered by their determination to resist darkness.

As the sunlight broke through the gloom, illuminating the chaos of their struggle, Liora knew they had found their footing in this realm—a place where humanity could transcend fear. Together, they stood steadfast, ready for whatever challenges awaited. The tide was turning; it was up to them to ensure that darkness would never reclaim their home.

All at once, the monsters that had loomed above them began to wane, not due to strength but the realization that they had underestimated the power of a united humanity. Liora felt hope burgeon in her chest, and in that crowded moment—filled with fatiguing breaths, bloodied hands, and the cries of persistent souls—she understood that, despite the chaos, humanity could emerge stronger than ever before.

As they regrouped after the encounter, hearts still pounding, friendships forged amongst the defense, Liora locked eyes with Ezekiel. They had accomplished something greater than mere survival. In the chaos of battle, they had stitched together not just a line of defense but a tapestry of hope that would resonate through the realms.

"Remember this moment," Ezekiel advised, his voice low yet filled with warmth. "This is only the beginning. Hold onto each other; it will guide you when darkness threatens again."

Liora nodded, understanding that their unity would forever be the cornerstone of their existence. They may have encountered monsters, but what emerged from that battle was something far more divine—a spirit forged in the fires of determination, sacrifice, and humanity's unwavering will.

The ultimate confrontation was still on the horizon, one that would shake the foundations of their worlds. But they were ready. No longer mere survivors, they had become warriors, bearers of light amidst shadow, prepared to reclaim their home from chaos.

Gathering again as a team—each heart brimming with resilience—they turned their sights toward the battles yet to come. In that unity, as souls intertwined in purpose, they would not falter. For they were humanity, and together, they would shine fiercely against the darkness.

The Turning Tide

With the horizon stained in hues of crimson and ash, the battlefield stretched before Seraphiel—an expanse of chaos where the lines between friend and foe blurred into insignificance. The tainted air hummed with the echoes of clashing wills, the sounds of desperation streaming from both the angelic and monstrous ranks. Humanity, caught in the crossfire, struggled to hold on to their fleeting moments of courage, their screams muffled beneath the weight of divine conflict.

Seraphiel flapped his wings, channeling streams of light that illuminated his surroundings, casting a stark contrast against the creeping shadows of despair that encroached upon the hearts of men and angels alike. His gaze scanned the scene; amidst the fray, he spotted Liora, her defiance reminiscent of a flickering flame against a vast ocean of darkness. But the weight of his own past decisions tugged at his heart, a relentless reminder that the battle was not merely a physical confrontation but an internal struggle against the remnants of his former self.

"Focus!" he commanded himself, shaking off the memories of warmth and harmony from the angelic realm. Each beat of his heart resonated with the pulse of the Earth beneath him, a reminder that every choice he had made contributed to this devastating war.

He had once stood at the vanguard of righteousness, revered as one of the highest seraphs until the call of freedom had lured him into rebellion. As the specter of chaos loomed ever larger, the walls he had built around his heart began to crumble, drawing him closer to the precipice of despair.

Across the battlefield, Azazel, his former comrade turned adversary, wielded chaos like a blade. The fallen angel radiated an aura of malevolence, reveling in the disorder he had sowed. He, too, saw the beauty in destruction, but his was a twisted appreciation for the havoc he had unleashed. A smirk played across his lips as he filled the air with dark energy, inciting fear and confusion among both mortals and angels. With each wave of his hand, he conjured nightmares—monsters ripped from the shadows to wreak havoc on any who dared defy him.

"Do you see the irony, Seraphiel?" Azazel's voice rang out, echoing through the tumult as if it were a ghost taunting its own grave. "You're fighting for a world that doesn't believe in you anymore! They're afraid of us; fear is a far stronger weapon than mere belief."

Seraphiel clenched his jaw, feelings of valor swirling in a tempest of doubt. "You've twisted what we once stood for, Azazel. This chaos isn't freedom; it's tyranny veiled in shadows. The mortals need hope, not nightmares!"

A low, mocking laughter erupted from Azazel, sending shivers up Seraphiel's spine. "Hope? We are the harbingers of change! They have long forgotten the light, embraced the darkness, and now—" his eyes glinted with malicious fervor, "now they must learn to appreciate it!"

The sentiment resonated through the battlefield like a ripple, catching the weary fighters off guard, and briefly halting the onslaught. For just a moment, individuals from both sides turned to contemplate the validity of these opposing views. Seraphiel's heart raced; could it be possible that the intertwining fates of heaven and hell drew the lines of good and evil into a delicate web?

As he wrestled with these thoughts, Liora emerged from the throng, her expression fierce yet uncertain. "We can't allow this conflict to escalate any further!" she shouted, her voice rising over the din. "There are lives at stake.

You both must see that this isn't just about you!"

Azazel's attention shifted towards her, and at that moment, something flickered behind his eyes—recognition. Perhaps it was the memory of humanity's resilience or the bond they once shared with those who long ago stopped believing in angelic divinity. But it was fleeting, tucked away by his arrogance as he dismissed her plea, calling it naïveté.

"Your heart longs for harmony in a world that is miserable and corrupted, girl," he sneered. "You've seen the light, and yet you crave the shadows. Embrace it, for you stand on the threshold of a new era!"

Yet, beneath his outward bravado, uncertainty lurked—a chink in his armor. Seraphiel saw it, that flicker of vulnerability that echoed his own inner conflict. It pushed him towards a new realization: perhaps the key to this battle lay not in steadfast positions of righteousness or malice but in understanding the gray that permeated the struggle.

"Azazel!" Seraphiel's voice rang out with newfound fervor, clarity slicing through the chaos fogging his thoughts. "What if we laid down our weapons and combined forces to battle a common enemy—the chaos that threatens all realms? There is a darkness more profound than any of us, one that binds us together. If we do not act now, we risk losing everything."

Liora's eyes widened, and behind her, the remaining soldiers of both factions paused, uncertainty weaving through their hearts as they contemplated the proposal that hung in the air. A delicate silence enveloped the chaos of battle, an inaudible gasp echoing between angels and monsters alike.

Azazel regarded him with those penetrating eyes, their depths fathomless—star-studded abysses reflecting the cosmos' unfathomable chaos. For once, a flicker of consideration ignited in his gaze, lingering just long enough for Seraphiel to seize the moment.

A heartbeat passed before Azazel scoffed, masking his hesitation with cold indifference. "You think I'd ally with the likes of you? You're a relic of a bygone age, clinging to illusions of honor and duty," he retorted, but there was a tremor of doubt in his voice.

Seraphiel took a step forward, his wings spreading wide, a display of vulnerability that felt foreign yet necessary. "And you, Azazel, are bound to the chaos that reshaped you. But deep down, we once were allies. We fought side by side against the very darkness that you now champion." His words hung in the air, begging for acknowledgment.

As tension coiled tighter, Liora interjected, her voice steady and firm. "No one wants this fight. We can create a new path—a way forward together! But we must do it united. If we fail to look beyond ourselves, we doom not just our realms, but everyone who dwells within them to an eternity of suffering."

The fire in her heart ignited the fading passions of truth within both unlikely allies. Azazel's smirk faltered as if cracking a mask on the verge of shattering. He shifted, tension rippling through his form, revealing a tempest of emotions residing behind his golden façade.

"Speak, then," Azazel ordered a subtle deepening of darkness in his voice, edging closer to agreement. "What do you suggest, Seraphiel?"

Seraphiel drew a deep breath; this was the pivotal moment. "Let us combine our strengths to confront the ancient evil that has awakened in our absence—the true monster that feeds on chaos and despair. This is our chance to redefine who we are, not as angels or monsters but as beings of the realms fighting for our combined futures. Let's cleanse our world together."

The murmurs of humans and celestial beings alike surged forth, with hearts fluttering at the prospect of unity. A delicate thread of hope wove itself through the air, pulsing like the heartbeat of the Earth itself beneath their feet, creating a tenuous bridge between the bloodied factions.

Yet doubt remained, clawing at Azazel's pride. "What guarantee do we have?" he challenged his voice a deep rumble of uncertainty. "What if your so-called redemption is nothing but a guise to restore the old order? You would have me return to the very chains I broke!"

Seraphiel met the glare of Azazel's fiery eyes with his own unwavering resolve. "Perhaps we both seek a new order transcending the chains from which we both long to be free."

In that moment, the battlefield held its breath. Time stilled, caught within the tension of possibilities shaping their destinies. Azazel's façade cracked further, revealing tumult brewing beneath—a tempest of doubt, regret, and the vague longing for his past.

"Then it shall be so," Azazel uttered finally, an uneasy alliance forged between shadows and light. His decision echoed through the battleground's silence, a ripple of shock and hope setting fire to the complexities of allegiance.

Angels and monsters stepped back as one, rallying around this newfound bond. Seraphiel felt the weight of the world lift as a wave of harmony swept through the air, plugging the bleeding wounds that had furrowed into their existence. Nature hummed in relief as the forces of chaos withdrew, turning to face the true enemy awakening within the heart of the realm.

Yet, as they stood together—two once-divided companions, now reluctant allies under a smoldering sky—Seraphiel felt the creeping encroachment of trepidation. The choice had been made, but would it be enough to alter the tides of war? The true threat loomed, one that stirred in the recesses of their collective memories, reminiscent of whispers from the time long before the fall.

And the final reality struck him—the moment filled with both dread and exhilaration. The balance of celestial realms depended on this fragile pact, their fates intertwining like roots in ancient trees beneath the Earth's surface. But beneath the surface of calm lay turbulent waters, stirred by the awakening monstrosity that challenged their union.

As they turned their attention toward the dark horizon, where shadows danced and flickered ominously, Liora's cry mingled with the warriors' heavy breathing on both sides, resonating with an electric charge. "Together, we stand, or we fall!"

Behind them, the lingering doubts still clung—the echoes of their pasts whispering fears of betrayal and ambition. Azazel's acceptance of Seraphiel's truth bore the weight of uncertainty, testing the fragile alliance as they prepared for the true confrontation ahead: an encroaching darkness that threatened to swallow each realm whole.

No one could yet foresee the tides that would truly turn—the consequences of their union and the fabric of fate so precariously woven.

As the smoke cleared, revealing an army of ancient terrors clawing towards them, hope, fear, and the unyielding entanglements of destiny coalesced in an unforgettable present—a moment just before the storm.

Here, in this grounded reality, the shadows and light gathered their energies, refashioning the celestial order into something entirely new, and the battle for Earth began anew.

6

Whispers of the Divine

Divine Communication

Liora awoke with the first light breaking through the heavy curtains of her small room. The dream lingered still, vivid and unsettling, as her heart raced to the rhythm of its imagery. Shadows danced at the edges of her vision, whispering secrets she could barely grasp. Each night felt like another chapter in a story she did not fully understand, yet one she feared she was destined to live out. This morning, however, the dream was particularly potent, a flicker of urgency igniting her spirit.

Sitting up, she thrust her fingers through her tousled hair . She took a moment to breathe deeply, grounding herself in the familiarity of the mundane: the coolness of the floor beneath her bare feet, the scent of fresh bread wafting from the kitchen, and the comforting hum of life outside her window. Yet, despite the warmth of her surroundings, a chill lingered in her bones—a reminder of the shadows from her dreams, the flickering images of the celestial and the monstrous that taunted her.

Her visions had begun simply enough—fragments of light and color, veiled truths that danced just beyond her reach. Yet, over time, they had grown more intense and more demanding. Each vision felt like an echo, a relay of thoughts from beyond her realm. They hinted at impending chaos, a disturbance echoing through the layers of reality that stretched thinly between her world and the celestial realms. She had learned to pay attention, to decipher the symbols that fluttered like moths caught in a storm. But this morning was different; the urgency echoed in her gut, begging her to take heed.

Liora pulled herself from her bed and shuffled toward her small desk. The rosewood surface was cluttered with sketches of symbols—spiraling shapes that twisted in on themselves and ancient runes that glowed with a faint luminescence. Each mark represented a vision recorded and interpreted, a thread in the tapestry of destiny that wound through her life. But today, as she rifled through her notes, something glimmered in her mind, a pressing need to piece together the fragments of her dreams before the light faded.

The images from last night drifted back to her like pollen carried by the wind. She had stood in a vast, shimmering field, the grass glistening as though it had captured the stars above. In the distance, a figure made of pure light emerged, a being whose wings fanned out in brilliant radiance, yet a shadow loomed behind them—dark, heavy, and menacing. The figure turned, and Liora felt an unshakable sense of familiarity as it beckoned her forward. But just as she reached out, a rift tore through the heavens, and monstrous laughter echoed.

Liora didn't want to remember the sound. It was harsh, chilling, and echoed with promises of doom. She had felt the dichotomy between hope and despair—a reminder that light and darkness were inextricably linked. But what did it mean? What was she to do with the essence of this vision creeping into her reality?

Taking a deep breath, Liora closed her eyes, allowing herself to sink into the afterglow of sleep. She let the sensation wash over her, hoping to capture the feeling of the dream once more, exploring its nuances. All at once, flashes of symbols slid into her consciousness: an eye, a scale, a feather, and a serpent. Each emblem tugged at her mind, begging her to understand their significance.

"Liora!" Her father's voice broke through her reverie, calling her down for breakfast. As always, his tone was warm yet firm, full of love laced with concern. He was a grounding presence, the anchor in her life, but even now, she felt the tangible pull of the celestial—the urgency coursing through her veins. "You'll miss the day if you keep dreaming!"

With a sigh, Liora opened her eyes. Today marked an important chapter in her understanding of the gifts she had been given, and lingering in bed wouldn't help unravel the riddle before her. "I'm coming!" she called, quickly sliding into her clothes and pushing her thoughts of the dream aside, if only temporarily.

As she joined her father in the kitchen, the delicious smell of freshly baked bread momentarily distracted her from her mental whirlwind. Her father, a man of humble stature with hands calloused by years of hard work, wore a patient smile. "You seem distracted again, my dear. Have you had another vision?"

The knowing glint in his eyes made Liora's stomach tighten. Her father understood her the best of all her family, recognizing that the shadows in her dreams held more than mere nightmares. They were messages, beckoning her to listen, to act. "Yes, but I'm still trying to understand it. I saw light, but there was darkness creeping close. And a rift..."

Her father's expression shifted, the warmth in his smile replaced by a shadow of concern. "The balance between light and darkness is a persistent struggle, Liora. You know that. But you mustn't lose yourself in the interpretation. Sometimes, the visions may serve as a warning, but they do not dictate your actions."

"But how can I ignore them?" she pressed, her voice rising. "If there are signs—"

"Then we must find the strength to respond." He paused, letting his words settle. "Remember, interpretations of visions can be as twisted as the nightmares themselves. When you find clarity, act upon it. Until then, I will be with you. Always."

Those words settled like a balm over her frayed nerves, an acknowledgment of her fears mixed with a profound comfort. But even with his understanding, she couldn't shake the weight of her visions. If they held truth, she had to confront it head-on, ready to embrace both the celestial whispers and the monstrous shadows.

Breakfast passed with similar banter—a mix of laughter and love that grounded her in the tangible. After confirming her plans for the day, Liora knew she had to seek solace at the old oak tree near the edge of the village. It was a sacred spot where she often came to connect with the earth and clear her mind. With its gnarled roots and sprawling branches, the tree seemed to pulse with ancient energy, as if it bore witness to the secrets whispered between realms.

As she walked through the village, murmurs of the past rustled in her mind. Stories of divine interventions and monstrous encounters echoed in her consciousness. Tales of Lumerian heroes and Galadrians—beings of luminescent light and shadows that walked among mortals—filled her thoughts. Humanity often failed to recognize the delicate line separating the divine from the monstrous, a reality that hung around her like a cloak. Liora felt a stirring deep within her, a desire to unravel the truth that connected them all.

Arriving at the old oak, Liora rested against its rough bark; the familiar scent of the earth calmed her restless spirit. She watched the sunlight filter through the leaves, casting intricate patterns upon the ground. Closing her eyes, she focused on her breath, the sounds of nature enveloping her, and urged the visions to come forth, surrendering herself to the divine communication she longed to understand.

What came next was a cacophony of sensation. Images erupted forth, vivid and colorful, spinning tales that intertwined their fates. She glimpsed other mortals—men and women, young and old—who bore their own burdens and secrets—a woman in a quiet room clutches a shimmered pendant—a sign of divine protection. A child watching a storm from the window, eyes wide with wonder, sensing an approaching danger. A soldier standing on the battlefield, his heart a battleground of fear and courage, contemplating the echoes of his choices. Each vision was clear, and each moment resonated with a truth transcending space and time.

Liora's consciousness reached out, threading through their stories, igniting a shared urgency. They, too, were connected, awakened by messages that called to them through dreams, whispers, and divine signs. Voices began to meld, speaking of hope and despair, bearing witness to the struggles of destinies colliding.

In the midst of this chaos, a new figure emerged—an old woman, face lined with wisdom, who looked deeply into Liora's soul. "You must listen, child," she urged, her voice barely a whisper. "The threads of fate are entwined, and your gift is both a blessing and a burden. Interpret wisely, for your choices will shape the world."

Suddenly, the visions shifted, the tranquil oak fading into darkness, the whispers growing louder. Shadows surged at the edges of her consciousness, echoing the laughter that haunted her dreams. In a moment of clarity, Liora recognized the embodiment of chaos lurking just beyond the realm of light, ready to seize the moment of confusion and harvest what fear would yield.

She pulled herself back effortlessly, gasping for breath as reality rushed back to her. The urgency was palpable, a palpable thread connecting the fate of many. Liora's heart drummed in her chest as she gathered her thoughts, recognizing the significance of her wandering mind. The chaos she had just witnessed was not simply a collection of moments; they were the crossroads of choice, compelling her to act upon their interconnected stories.

She understood that divine communication was not solely about receiving visions or dreams but about the responsibility of those who heard them. Wherever the stories from the celestial wrought futures that collided with the mundane, she felt a duty—a duty to bridge the gap between the realms and unite the threads of fate, urging those she glimpsed to embrace their roles in the prophecy unfolding around them.

Liora felt a spark of resolve igniting within her as the sun dipped lower in the sky, painting the world in shades of gold. She must return to the village, gather those whose fates intertwined with hers, and share what she had learned—a beacon of hope amidst the darkness, ready to guide others who stood on the precipice of their destinies.

Unknowingly, she began to walk, her steps hurried yet purposeful as anticipation thrummed through her veins. She would seek the others touched by the divine, those who felt the pull of visions but had yet to recognize the significance of their gifts. Liora would not stand alone; she would weave their stories together, igniting the dim embers of realization that could illuminate their path forward.

With every moment carrying her closer to this mission, she reached for her heart, her pulse quickening as she considered the threads yet to be woven. She wouldn't allow fear to stifle her voice as darkness loomed on the horizon. Instead, with fervor burning within her soul, she would embrace her role as a harbinger of the celestial, eager to listen and act.

"Divine whispers," she murmured softly, her spirit aflame with purpose. "Unite us, guide us, and reveal our destiny." And thus began her journey—a quest to interpret the divine messages that would illuminate the path ahead while navigating the complexities that lay between the realms of light and darkness. As the stars twinkled in the dusk sky, Liora stepped forward, ready to embrace her fate, determined to decipher the whispers that forged her destiny.

The Role of the Oracle

The air buzzed with anticipation as Liora stood at the threshold of the Oracle's domain. A pervading mist cloaked the ancient grove, the subtle hum of energy palpable as she took her first step inside. It felt as if she were crossing into another realm altogether, one where time flowed differently, marked not by the clocks of humanity but by the pulsing rhythm of the cosmic heartbeat.

The grove was serene yet charged, each leaf shimmering with an ethereal light. Tall trees, their trunks twisted and gnarled by centuries of wisdom, loomed overhead. Sunlight filtered through the canopy, casting a kaleido-scope of shadows and glimmers upon the ground. In the heart of this mystical grove lay an ornate altar draped in silken fabrics, flowers blooming in hues vibrant enough to rival the heavens. Liora felt her pulse quicken as she caught sight of a figure seated at the altar, shrouded in a flowing robe that seemed to blend seamlessly with the surrounding nature.

"Do you seek the truth, young seer?" the Oracle's voice rang out, soft yet resonant, echoing through the grove like a distant melody. It was more a feeling than a sound, wrapping around her heart and easing her apprehensions. The Oracle's presence was magnetic, a paradox of warmth and otherworldliness that pulled Liora closer.

"I—" Liora stammered, her heart racing at the weight of the moment. "I seek answers... about the prophecy, about what's to come."

A knowing smile spread across the Oracle's face but did not reach her eyes, which bore the weight of unfathomable knowledge. "Prophecies are threads woven into the tapestry of existence, shaping destinies yet to be, but beware—knowledge is a double-edged sword. It enlightens and burdens."

Liora swallowed hard. She could already feel the weight of the prophecy pressing against her chest. It was as if the very air grew thicker with every word spoken. "I need to know. We need to prepare. The realms are on the brink of war, and these visions... they only bring more questions."

The Oracle inclined her head, acknowledging Liora's pain. "The visions you bear are not mere whims of the cosmos; they are whispers of the divine, echoes of potential futures. Seek the truth in these whispers, but tread softly, for the burden of foresight can twist your heart."

Before Liora could respond, a rustling sound echoed through the grove. Ezekiel, her steadfast guardian, emerged from the shadows, his expression a blend of concern and determination. "Liora," he said, his voice steady. "Is everything—"

"She will learn what must be learned," the Oracle interrupted, her gaze unwavering as it shifted to Ezekiel. "Though the paths they tread intersect, the choices made will differ. Yet, all lead toward the same horizon."

Ezekiel frowned slightly. "What do you mean?"

"The proximity of turmoil draws together beings of light and shadow," the Oracle explained, her eyes glinting with the flicker of celestial light. "The realms entwine, yet fate dances upon the precipice of chaos. Your bond will be tested, as will your convictions."

Liora's heart raced as she exchanged a fleeting look with Ezekiel—a silent understanding passed between them. How many futures hung in the balance? The love they nurtured amidst darkness was a beacon in tumultuous times, but would it withstand the trials ahead?

"Will the burden of this prophecy drive us apart?" Liora whispered, her voice catching in her throat. "Will choosing to follow our destinies tear us asunder?"

The Oracle's expression softened momentarily. "All relationships are tested by the gravity of choice. Only through understanding the essence of your soul can you weather the storms that lie ahead. You will have to decide: will you cling to what was, or will you dare to forge what is to come?"

Ezekiel stepped forward, his posture protective, determined. "We will face whatever comes—together."

The Oracle nodded, her enigmatic smile returning. "Ah, together. A powerful word drenched in meaning. Take heed, for the ties you forge and the choices you make will resound through the fabric of the realms. The threads you create will bind not just you but all that is and will be."

"Tell us what we need to know," Liora pressed, her voice a blend of desperation and resolve. "Please. We have to understand this prophecy."

A heavy silence enveloped the grove. The Oracle's eyes glimmered with an inscrutable depth as if they were windows into the cosmos itself. "Very well. Listen closely, for the essence of prophecy is clarity woven with uncertainty."

As the Oracle began to speak, tendrils of shimmering magic coalesced around her hands, swirling with a vibrant aura. Liora and Ezekiel leaned closer, their breaths bated.

"It is foretold that a cataclysmic convergence shall awaken the slumbering monsters among men, etching despair into the hearts of the innocent." The Oracle's voice resonated with a haunting quality. "Yet, from this chaos, a choice will arise. A choice that holds the power to restore balance or plunge the realms into deeper darkness."

"What does that choice entail?" Liora asked, sensing the dread woven within the words.

"The choice is yours, Liora." The Oracle's gaze pierced through her soul. "To embrace your lineage's destiny or reject the divine's call. Each path leads to divergent endings, but the cost shall be great."

"What lineage?" Liora's heart raced, unease welling within her.

"The blood of the celestial runs deep within you," the Oracle stated, her voice firm yet ethereal. "You are not merely a mortal, Liora. You are a bridge— a connector between realms. Your embrace of this truth could alter the fate of all."

Ezekiel stepped forward protectively, his brow furrowing. "What do you mean?"

"The gifts bestowed upon her are not merely blessings," the Oracle explained, the atmosphere thickening with significance. "They are burdens wrapped in celestial light, beckoning at the edge of her consciousness. Weigh your decisions carefully, for they will reverberate beyond your comprehension—a dance of destiny entwined with choice."

Liora's mind raced. Was she truly more than merely human? Could she bring forth the change needed to heal the realm, or was she destined to become a vessel of destruction? The prospect filled her with both wonder and trepidation.

"Your confusion is evident," the Oracle continued, unfazed by Liora's internal strife. "Embrace this uncertainty, for only through the struggle may you uncover your purpose. The truths born of choices are not always as they seem; reality forms around the beliefs you hold dear. Keep your heart open."

Without a moment to process the Oracle's words, the air grew tense, the grove humming with energy not confined to nature. Shadows elongated, curling like smoke, and for an instant, Liora thought she saw specters ripple through the trees. Visions of battles fought, lost loves, and creatures lurking just beyond the veil flashed before her eyes, overwhelming her senses.

"It is time for you both to witness," the Oracle spoke, her voice an anchor in the surging tide of visions. "What lies beneath the surface, the choices made, and the consequences borne from them."

As Liora's vision blurred, she felt herself slipping beyond her physical body, her consciousness awash with glimpses of futures not yet realized. She stood in a vast realm, filled with light and harmony but marred by rotten shadows creeping at the edges, encroaching upon the brilliance like a plague.

Time flowed like a rushing river, and Liora was swept away, witnessing a myriad of lives unfold. She saw towns lost to war, hearts shattered by betrayal, and souls twisted by ambition. She felt the weight of despair echo through her, resonating with her own worries and dreams. But amidst the turmoil, she glimpsed flashes of hope—acts of courage, moments of unity that ignited a spark within her.

The pulse of choice became a clarion call. A line drawn in the sand—would she become a harbinger of chaos or a beacon of hope? The weight of the universe rested upon that decision, and the knowledge made her heart ache with both dread and exhilaration.

"Liora," Ezekiel's voice pierced the haze, pulling her back to the sanctuary of the grove. "You're with me. We're here together."

She gasped, the relentless stream of visions receding as she returned to the present reality. The Oracle watched, an enigmatic smile touching her lips. "This is but a fragment of what is to come, young seer. The path remains unwritten, shaped by the intentions you harbor. Trust in your instincts, for they are your greatest guide."

Breathlessly, Liora turned to Ezekiel. "Did you see it? The choices... the lives—"

"Shh," Ezekiel whispered, placing a steadying hand on her shoulder. "You don't need to explain it now. What matters is what you will do with this knowledge. We can't shy away from the burden of these revelations."

"But what if I don't know how?" Liora felt despair creeping in like a chill, her vision of light dimmed by self-doubt. "What if I'm just a human standing against the tide of fate?"

The Oracle's gaze softened as she stepped closer, the trees bending slightly as if drawn by her presence. "Remember, Liora, even the smallest of choices can shift the balance of entire realms. You are not merely acting on your own power; you are part of a greater narrative, a web of choices connected across all beings."

Ezekiel's eyes gleamed with determination as he gazed at Liora, "Whatever happens, we face it together. You must trust in us."

"Indeed," the Oracle chimed, her voice resonant with unwavering conviction. "The time for action approaches swiftly. You stand at the crossroads, but remember that fate favors the courageous. Every choice you make is a brushstroke on the canvas of your destiny."

As her words echoed in the air, a palpable energy swirled around them, shifting the atmosphere once again. The Oracle continued, her form radiating an almost tangible light, "Seek clarity amongst the tides of confusion, embrace your heritage, and remember—darkness cannot exist without light. Brave the tempest, and through unity, you may discover the key to transcendence."

With urgency sparking in their hearts, Liora and Ezekiel exchanged one resolute glance. The fear mingling with hope ignited a commitment within them, something forged in the fires of their trials. Prophecy or not, they would stand together against the coming storm.

"Thank you," Liora murmured, her heart swelling with newfound purpose. "We will face what lies ahead."

The Oracle bowed her head in acknowledgment as the mist began to thicken around them. "The time for reckoning draws near. Prepare well, young ones, for the whispers of destiny grow ever louder."

And with that, Liora and Ezekiel stepped back from the celestial grove, the heavy weight of prophecy still lingering in their minds but now entwined with the light of hope they would carry into the world. Together, they would traverse the delicate threads woven through realms, forging their own path, guided by unity and purpose, determined to rewrite the fate awaiting them amidst the shadows of impending chaos.

Interpreting the Signs

The sun hung low in the sky, casting long shadows across the landscape as Liora sat in the quiet grove where she often retreated for solace. The air was tinged with the scent of blooming jasmine, but the beauty of her surroundings now seemed overshadowed by the turmoil brewing within her heart. The visions had come again—vivid and unrelenting, pulling her deeper into the web of destiny she was meant to unravel. She clenched her hands into fists, digging her nails into her palms as if to anchor herself against the tide of uncertainty that threatened to sweep her away.

Her mind wandered back to the last vision: an ancient battlefield where brilliant light clashed against encroaching darkness. Shadows of demons danced around the edges, their grotesque forms twisting violently in the chaos, while radiant figures fought to protect the flickering flame of hope that lay at the center. But what had struck her most was the face of a fallen angel—Seraphiel, his expression a blend of anguish and determination. He had looked directly at her, his lips moving, but the words were lost in the roar of battle. Even now, the memory of his fierce gaze haunted her, compelling her to understand.

Liora pulled a deep breath into her lungs, seeking to steady the whirlwind of emotions within her. She closed her eyes, recalling the words from her dream: "In the unraveling, find the thread that binds." What did it mean? What thread was she supposed to find? The visions connected her to something greater but left her more confused than enlightened. Each revelation felt like a weight pressing on her, demanding her to act, but she was left with more questions than answers.

Her thoughts shifted to Ezekiel, her guardian angel who had helped her navigate her sporadic encounters with the divine. She had devised a plan to meet him tonight in the forest, far from prying eyes. There, under the cloak of darkness, she hoped to find clarity amidst her doubts. The alignment of stars she had witnessed in her visions felt significant, and perhaps he could help her interpret their meaning.

As the light began to fade, Liora rose and made her way through the underbrush, her heart pounding with anticipation and trepidation. The path wound along the edge of a bubbling brook, the sound of its water a gentle reminder of nature's constancy. Yet, she knew that this was a world poised on the brink of chaos—an impending clash of realms where the fate of humanity hung delicately in the balance.

When she arrived at their meeting place, the night sky was blanketed with stars, shimmering like countless watchful eyes. She stood quietly, feeling the energy shift around her as if the universe itself was holding its breath. Moments later, she sensed Ezekiel's presence before he materialized before her, his ethereal form glowing softly in the dim light. Though folded, his wings seemed to shimmer with celestial energy, making him seem otherworldly and achingly familiar.

"Liora," he greeted her, his voice smooth and comforting like the first breezes of spring. "You summoned me."

"I need your guidance," she admitted, feeling her courage falter. "The visions are growing more intense. I can't decipher them. Every time I think I have a handle on their meaning, something's thrown back in my face."

Ezekiel nodded knowingly, stepping closer, the warmth of his presence enveloping her. "Your gifts are both a blessing and a burden. It is natural to feel overwhelmed, especially when the stakes are high. Tell me of your latest vision."

With a deep breath, Liora recounted the imagery of the battlefield—the brutal clash between light and dark, the demons, and Seraphiel's tortured expression. The words flowed from her like a dam bursting, each detail painting a vivid portrait of the urgency that consumed her.

"So many of them were fighting, but it felt like the light was fighting for something more than just victory," she explained, her voice trembling. "As if there was a reason beyond mere survival. And then, there was him—Seraphiel. It's like he was trying to reach me, but I couldn't grasp what he wanted."

Ezekiel listened intently, the gentle furrow of his brow deepening with her distress. "Seraphiel fights against the darkness within himself, Liora. He bears the weight of his choices—a burden I know all too well. In your visions, there is a message woven into the chaos. The light he represents is hope, even in the darkest of times."

"But what hope is there for someone who has fallen so far?" she questioned, her heart throbbing against her ribs. "If he is lost, what chance does that leave for us? What chance does that leave for me?" The self-doubt seeped through, and Liora felt the weight of her potential collapsing onto her.

Ezekiel stepped forward, pressing a comforting hand onto her shoulder. "Every soul carries the potential for redemption. It is your role to help him see that hope doesn't fade; it only transforms. Keep the faith, Liora. The signs will guide you, but you must be willing to interpret their meanings rather than surrendering to despair."

"What if I fail? What if my interpretations only lead to more chaos?" The panic bubbled within her, but she could also feel the resolve beginning to shimmer beneath it like the first rays of dawn. She understood that this was not just about Seraphiel; it was about her, too.

"You are not alone in this, nor are you without purpose," he assured her. "The threads woven together create a tapestry of fate that binds us all. Seek the meaning beyond the vision itself. The signs may be obscure, yet their essence lies within your heart, waiting to guide you."

Encouraged by his words, Liora nodded, though doubt still creased her brow. "I will try. I want to understand. I want to know how to help."

As the weight of her vision faded into determination, Ezekiel took a step back, his entire demeanor transforming, radiating an energy both fierce and gentle. "The signs will come more clearly, but you must remain open to interpretation. They may not reveal themselves immediately, and some truths could be painful. Can you bear that weight?"

"I can," she whispered, feeling the fire of her resolve ignite within her. "I need to."

"Then listen closely," he began, his voice lowering to a near-reverent tone. "You must quiet your mind and trust your instincts. The signs will come in many forms—through nature, dreams, and even in the conversations you hold. Remain vigilant and aware, for the clearest messages may lie in the most subtle gestures."

Once again, she drew in a shaky breath, determination solidifying in her chest. "I will."

As they spoke, the distant sound of thunder echoed, and Liora felt a shiver race down her spine, sensing the ripple of energy in the air. The winds shifted, and she looked up to see dark clouds gathering ominously on the horizon. Her heart quickened; the signs were manifesting faster than she anticipated. Something was coming, and they would not have much time before the storm broke.

"Liora, the time for action grows near," Ezekiel warned, his expression grave and focused. "Unlike before, the weight of the destiny you hold is heavier now, and it will demand clarity and courage to see it through."

"I know," Liora replied, her voice stronger now. "What can I do?"

He searched her gaze, intense and bright but tinged with worry. "You must gather the knowledge and prepare as best you can. Find others who walk the delicate line between realms. Their insights could illuminate the truths you seek. And, above all else, trust what you feel when the moments arrive."

With a newfound sense of purpose, Liora nodded fervently, each affirmation laced with fierce commitment. The storm mirrored the tumult within, but now she felt ready to face it.

As they exchanged lingering glances, a blinding flash illuminated the sky, followed by a resounding crack of thunder that seemed to shake the very ground beneath them. The air was electric with foreboding, but Liora stood her ground instead of recoiling, bolstered by the conviction that now surged through her veins.

"Go, Liora," Ezekiel urged, taking a step back. "Seek the signs, unravel their meaning, and prepare yourself for what lies ahead. Your destiny awaits, and it is time to embrace it."

Before she could respond, the wind picked up around them, swirling like a whirlwind that enveloped their surroundings. In the whirlwind, she found herself alone in the grove, breathless and invigorated by the gravity of what she had just experienced. The night felt deeper now, and she knew the moment to act had indeed arrived.

Liora turned toward the path that led back into the world, and determination etched on her countenance. As she stepped away from the protective embrace of the grove, the sky thundered again, but this time her heart beat to the rhythm of resolve rather than fear. She felt the intensity of the divine at her back, propelling her forward.

In the days that followed, Liora sought the counsel of the wise. She approached scholars and mystics, weaving through the crowded markets and secretive alleys where whispers of the divine floated in the air like smoke. Each encounter brought new perspectives—stories of prophetic dreams, celestial alignments, and the interconnectedness of existence.

Yet, despite the wisdom she gained, Liora found herself grappling with uncertainty. Each sign held layers of complexities that would not easily yield their secrets. She often returned to the forest, seeking the solitude of the grove to meditate on the messages she deciphered. In those moments of quiet reflection, she began to understand the thread, the essence of what she was fighting for.

During one such session, she was struck by the image of the battlefield once again—the clashing forces playing out in her mind like a vivid tapestry. A strange sensation washed over her as she mused on the shared plight between Seraphiel and herself, the weight of the fallen crushing her spirit despite their differences. "The thread that binds," she whispered as shards of insight flashed through her consciousness. "Hope intertwines with regret and redemption."

Beneath it all lay something vital, a yearning for the light, not just for herself but for every being caught in the throes of conflict. Perhaps, she thought, it wasn't about deciphering every nuance but rather embracing the epic struggle for meaning that connected them all.

With this new understanding, Liora returned to the marketplace—a vibrant hub where people mingled, shared the news, and whispered tales of the celestial and monstrous. The urgency of the impending storm loomed over them like a dark cloud, and she could feel the electric anxiety of the crowd. She stepped forward, her voice steady as she began to speak, grabbing the attention of those nearby.

"Our world stands at the precipice of chaos," she declared, each word carrying the weight of her conviction. "The realms of angels and monsters threaten to collide. We are all woven into this narrative, bound by the hope that flickers within. We are not alone; the signs are here for us to interpret together."

Eyes widened with concern and curiosity as people leaned closer, drawn by her passion. "But how do we decipher our roles in this," a voice called. "Can we trust what we see, what we feel?"

"Trust your heart," Liora urged. "The signs manifest within us, guiding our actions even amid uncertainty. It is belief and conviction that will guide us toward our fate."

Her words resonated within the crowd, igniting whispers that ebbed and flowed like waves. The gathering pulse of hope surged between them, unifying their fears and aspirations into one unbroken chain. This connection fueled her strength, propelling her toward a greater purpose.

Days turned into nights, and each encounter nourished Liora's burgeoning natural instincts while tightening the invisible thread that indelibly bound their fates together. She received further visions—flashes of moments that embodied the struggles of those she had met, elevating their individual stories into a collective saga. In her dreams, she heard echoes of Seraphiel calling to her from the depths of shadows.

Then, without warning, she was awoken one night by a vision that sent chills through her. Seraphiel stood before her, surrounded by swirling darkness, but his expression bore an intensity that struck her to her core. "Find the thread, Liora. In the darkness, seek the light."

Stirred from sleep, Liora understood. The time had come to take that message to others. The fear of failure still lingered like a shadow at the corners of her mind, but she could no longer afford to let it control her destiny. Embracing the courage forged in the fires of her struggles, she began organizing a gathering in the heart of their town—where she had spoken with the crowd.

The urgency was palpable as she brought together those who had journeyed with her, individuals defined by their unique gifts and experiences. That night, under the stars, they shared their stories, their fears, and their insights, singing songs interlaced with the melodies of hope.

As laughter echoed amongst them and the warmth of camaraderie surrounded her, Liora felt the embers within her soul surge into flames. It was here that she realized that they would forge the connections necessary to face the coming storm. Each character, each story, was a piece of the larger tapestry, and somehow, she held the thread.

And then, as they formed a circle beneath the canopy of stars, Liora took a deep breath, the words coming as if written upon her heart. "We stand on the brink, but we are not helpless. We will interpret the signs together as a united front. We'll be stronger than we ever thought possible."

The energy crackled in the air, a beautiful tide of resilience swelling within them.

As they each took turns expressing their hopes, fears, and visions, traditions past and present, collided, one by one. They began to weave a plan—a spell of unity against the impending chaos. Liora felt exhaustion wash over her, but each exchange pulled her deeper into the purpose she had carried for so long.

It was only as the night waned that Liora realized the battle was far from concluded. Yet she understood now that though they faced turbulent waters, none of them would traverse them alone. Together, they could interpret the signs, unveil the messages hidden in the chaos, and perhaps unite the realms before the storm tested their courage.

And, perhaps most importantly, the moment of clarity she had prayed for had arrived. At last, she could act against the shadows that sought to conquer hope. She could embrace the significance of her destiny, and thus, she emerged strong, ready to meet the chaos that would soon unfurl. The weight of responsibility was still there, yet this time, it did not feel like a burden—it felt like a call to arms.

7

The Prophecy of Realms

The Unveiling

In the heart of the twilight hour, when the boundary between the realms thinned, Liora found herself in the sacred glade where the Oracle would often share her wisdom. The air tingled with a sense of reverence, an electricity that made the hair on the back of her neck stand on end. The landscape shimmered—trees stood sentinel, their leaves illuminated as if lit from within, while ethereal mist swirled at their roots. It felt like stepping into another world entirely, a place where truths beyond comprehension dwelled.

She wasn't alone. Ezekiel and Seraphiel stood by her side, their expressions a mix of determination and trepidation. The impending gathering felt monumental, the weight of destiny pressing upon them all. The Oracle, a figure cloaked in flowing veils that seemed to shift with the light, appeared before them. Her features were both ageless and timeless, her eyes deep pools of ancient knowledge that sparkled with the wisdom of untold epochs.

"Welcome, seekers of truth," the Oracle's voice echoed, resonating with the harmony of celestial spheres. "You have come to hear the whispers of fate, the echoes of a prophecy that intertwines your destinies with the tapestry of existence."

Liora's heart raced. The words sent shivers down her spine. She had heard the rumors, the tales of a prophecy that could alter the fates of angels, humans, and beasts alike—prophecies that held the potential for both salvation and destruction. But to witness it unveiled? That was something else entirely.

"What is this prophecy?" she asked, her voice steady despite the turbulence within. "What must we know?"

The Oracle lifted her hands, and the air crackled with energy. "Listen closely. The prophecy of realms is not a simple string of words; it is a living truth that evolves and grows as the worlds turn. It warns of a time when the skies will darken, a time when alliances will shift like sand, and hearts will be tested in ways you cannot yet grasp."

A soft breeze rustled through the glade, carrying the scents of distant lands. Liora exchanged glances with Ezekiel, whose eyes reflected the same mix of hope and fear that churned within her. Seraphiel, standing with an air of noble resolve, seemed to channel a hint of certainty amidst the uncertainty.

The Oracle began to recite a series of enigmatic verses, and as she spoke, the very fabric of time seemed to warp. Words spilled forth like droplets of rain on parched earth:

"When light casts shadows long and deep,
    In the silence, the secrets keep.
    Beware the ties that bind too close,
    For trust and betrayal, a fragile dose.

From the ashes of the fallen gods,
    The choice of humanity is wrought with odds.
    Heroes will rise from deep despair,
    While monsters awaken from slumber rare.

In the balance of fate, the scales will tilt,
    As prophecy weaves the threads of guilt.
    A heart torn asunder shall find its voice,
    And in unity's strength, a rebirth of choice."

As the final words lingered in the air, a profound silence enveloped them. Liora's heart thudded painfully in her chest. Each line resonated deeply, a reflection of her own fears and aspirations. What did it mean? What ties would bind too close? The shadows of betrayal loomed large in her thoughts, especially in light of the growing tensions between realms.

Ezekiel, his brow furrowed in contemplation, broke the silence. "The choice of humanity... It suggests that our actions will dictate what comes next." He looked at Liora, their connection palpable. "We have to be prepared for whatever is coming."

Seraphiel stepped forward, his celestial grace illuminating the glade. "This prophecy speaks of heroes and monsters. We must understand our roles, for we have walked the line between both since the dawn of our existence. Liora, you may be the key to unraveling the truth. Your visions have always guided you, and your heart is intertwined with this prophecy."

Liora felt the weight of Seraphiel's words. The truth pressed down like a heavy mantle. "But how do we piece it together?" she asked, her voice trembling. "What can we do to change what is foretold?"

The Oracle moved closer, her presence both calming and electrifying. "To gather the threads is to seek understanding—each of you must confront your own choices and fears and embrace your truths. The path won't be easy; alliances will be tested, and sacrifices may be required. But in that struggle, you will find clarity."

The Oracle's words echoed in Liora's heart. Clarity. That was what she sought amid the swirling chaos of destiny. But what sacrifices awaited? What truths lay unacknowledged between her and her companions? Each had their battle, their secrets lodged like thorns in the soul. As Liora reflected on the Oracle's teachings, she realized they were inextricably tied not just by friendship, but by the burdens they carried.

The atmosphere in the glade shifted; the air grew heavier, charged with anticipation. Liora's gaze turned to the Oracle, who stood patiently, awaiting questions. "Can you tell us more about the ashes of the fallen gods?" she implored. "Are they connected to the monsters that roam our lands?"

At this inquiry, the Oracle's eyes darkened momentarily, shadows flickering across her face like the wisps of forgotten memories. "The fallen gods are remnants of rebellion," she explained, her voice laced with gravitas. "Angelic beings who traded their glories for the intoxicating lure of mortal desires. These beings now serve as harbingers of doom or salvation, depending on whose hands wield their destinies. It is a cycle that bleeds through realms."

"And what of the heroes?" Ezekiel interjected. "Are they truly born from despair, or do they emerge from within?"

"They will emerge," the Oracle replied with unwavering assurance. "Heroes are forged in the crucible of hardship; they arise from the ashes of despair to bring forth light amidst the darkness. But remember, the heart is both a source of strength and vulnerability. The choice to become a hero or a monster will ultimately lie within each soul."

Seraphiel's expressive eyes bore into Liora's, as if he could see the whirlpool of thoughts swirling within her mind. "This is our moment, Liora. We must unite our strengths if we are to face the chaos that unfolds. Your connection to both divine and mortal realms gives you a unique perspective."

Liora felt a spark of light within her heart as she contemplated the enormity of the Oracle's prophecy, but the flicker of fear still loomed. "And if we fail?"

The Oracle stepped closer, enveloping them in her presence. "The winds of fate are fickle. Though the darkness may be overwhelming, the light can still pierce through. But action is required. Trust in one another, for together you will decipher the meaning behind the celestial songs of the ancients."

With renewed determination, Liora sensed a resolve blossoming within her. "Then we must start now. We have to gather information, allies, and understand the implications of this prophecy before the shadows claim us all." Her words were filled with fervor, the urgency palpable in the gathering dusk.

Ezekiel nodded, his expression firm. "Every clue counts. The frayed threads of prophecy will lead us to the truth. Perhaps legends have something to tell us, tales of those who walked similar paths. It's time we seek them out."

Seraphiel's voice echoed like a clarion call. "Let's explore the histories of the fallen gods. The more we know about our adversaries, the better equipped we will be to combat the darkness that looms. For understanding, one's enemy is as important as knowing oneself."

The Oracle regarded them with pride, her ethereal light softening as she nodded. "Your resolve gives me hope. Seek the truth, for it lies in both ancient texts and the echoes of the past. Each step forward will illuminate the path ahead. But remember, the heart of the prophecy also lies within your connections to one another—you must nurture those bonds."

A hushed stillness enveloped the glade, the air thick with the weight of understanding. With the Oracle's cryptic insights echoing in their minds, they felt the gravity of the impending conflict drawing nearer, each heartbeat resonating with purpose.

Tension hung in the air as Liora felt a swirl of emotions—fear, determination, and a burgeoning hope. As they began formulating their plan and breaking from the Oracle's ethereal embrace, she felt a shift course through her thoughts. Prophecy wasn't merely fate laid bare; it was a reflection of choices, intertwined destinies, and the resolve to weather the storm.

As moonlight filtered through the trees and bathed the glade in silver, Liora turned to her companions, her heart brimming with conviction. "Let's uncover the stories of those before us. We must find our place among them, for the time of reckoning is upon us."

And as they turned to leave, each step was marked with purpose. Together, they would unravel the threads of prophecy, piece together the fragments of their destinies, and confront the shadows that threatened to swallow their worlds whole.

With every heartbeat, the prophecy loomed larger in their minds—the unfolding tapestry of realms, the shifting allegiances, and the age-old battle between light and darkness. Liora could sense that the path before them would be fraught with challenges, yet she walked forward with her companions, ready to forge their own destinies amidst the stars and shadows.

Little did they know, the revelation of the prophecy had only just begun. The significance of their choices echoed through time, and with every moment, it pulled them deeper into the unfolding saga that could reshape the very essence of the realms. The final confrontations awaited them, and as the winds whispered secrets of fate, they prepared to step into the path that would ultimately define their legacy.

The Impending Cataclysm

The air crackled with tension as Liora stood at the edge of the clearing, the remnants of a storm swirling around her like a tempest of uncertainty. The whispers of the prophecy echoed in her mind, weaving through the chaos like a specter, haunting yet compelling. All around her, the gathered beings—a motley assembly of angels, humans, and creatures of shadow—strained toward the words of the Oracle, each face a canvas painted with fear, hope, and desperation.

"What does it mean?" a voice murmured, cutting through the din. It was Ezekiel, his brows furrowed with the weight of his role as a guardian. "A cataclysm that threatens all realms... How can we prepare for such a thing?"

The Oracle, cloaked in mystery, stood at the center of the gathering, her voice a melodic chime that resonated with ethereal authority. "The cataclysm is not a singular event, but a convergence of choices," she explained, her eyes shimmering like stars in a velvet sky. "Each realm teeters on the edge of its destiny, and your actions will tip the balance."

Liora swallowed hard, her heart racing. What was she meant to do? The visions, once a source of wonder, now loomed as a heavy burden, laden with the reality of her part in this unfolding drama. With the fate of multiple realms hanging in the balance, the stakes were impossibly high.

"How do we fight against fate?" she asked, her voice trembling despite her efforts to sound resolute. "What if our choices only lead to more chaos?"

The Oracle's gaze softened, and for a moment, Liora glimpsed a flicker of understanding—a bond forged in the fires of shared destiny. "You are not meant to fight against fate, child," she replied gently. "Instead, you must understand it, embrace it. You cannot escape the choices laid before you, but you can choose how to respond."

As the haunting implications of the Oracle's words took root, a ripple of anxiety spread through the gathered assembly. A palpable tension hung in the air; each being grappling with their fears and aspirations. The dark abyss of uncertainty loomed ahead, beckoning them to face it, yet each of them was acutely aware of their own moral dilemmas.

"What is the point?" Azazel interjected, his voice smooth yet laced with an undercurrent of mischief. "The realms are already fragmented, teetering on disaster. Why should we fight against the inevitable? Embrace the chaos… it is liberating."

Several angels recoiled at his words, a flurry of gasps rippling through the crowd. Seraphiel stepped forward, his expression grim. "You think chaos is the answer?" he challenged, a mixture of fury and pity burning in his eyes. "You once knew the light, Azazel. We were created to uphold the divine order, not to revel in destruction."

But Azazel only smirked, the shadow of his past clinging to him like a second skin. "And what has that order brought us, my friend? Stagnation, oppression… the illusion of control. Embrace the freedom that chaos offers!"

Liora felt the conflict between them—two sides of the same coin, desperately seeking answers but arriving at vastly different conclusions. Her heart raced at the enormity of it all. She was a mere fragment in this cosmic tapestry, yet everything felt intricately connected.

As the argument escalated, Liora closed her eyes, attempting to force the tempest of emotions swirling around her into clarity. Images flickered through her mind: the quaint village she had grown up in, the laughter of children, the warmth of sun-drenched fields. And yet, she knew that such serenity could not last; the prophecy had forewarned upheaval and conflict.

Suddenly, Liora's vision shifted—a storm-clouded sky, crackling with energy. In the distance, beyond a jagged horizon, she saw a figure emerging from the darkness, a silhouette against the chaos. "We are the architects of our destinies," a voice echoed, strong and unwavering. It radiated conviction, reverberating through her mind and heart.

"Liora! Liora!" Ezekiel's voice broke through her reverie. Panic returned as she opened her eyes to find him kneeling before her, his expression a tumult of concern and urgency. "Are you with us?"

"Yes, I—" she stammered, grateful for his presence, though the weight of the prophecy still pressed heavily upon her chest.

"The rising tensions...the darkness encroaching..." he began, his face earnest. "We cannot afford to falter. The choices we make now will shape the future. It might seem bleak, but we must find a way to unify our realms."

The emotions swirling inside her surged to the forefront, and she realized it was time to choose—time to embrace her own destiny, no matter how daunting. "You're right," she breathed, an ember of determination igniting within her. "We must stand together if we are to prevent the impending cataclysm."

"Together..." She echoed those words, and as they departed her lips, a wave of hope washed over her. Was this the answer? The only way to counter the chaos of their worlds was to forge an unbreakable bond against it.

A ripple of agreement circulated through the gathered beings, and even Azazel paused, his expression faltering as he caught sight of the unity forming among them. A flicker of something—fear?—crossed his features, and Liora seized upon it.

"You've chosen to walk a path of darkness, Azazel, but that doesn't mean you can't turn back," she urged, hope coursing through her words. "Each of us has the choice to embrace either chaos or harmony. Do not surrender to despair."

"You speak of hope, Liora, yet the weight of the prophecy is suffocating," he countered, bitterness lacing his voice. "What if I were to reject this farcical notion of unity? Would that not render your words meaningless?"

"Rejecting unity only deepens the chasm between us," Liora replied, her voice steady. "We cannot afford to let fear dictate our choices. We must confront it together, embracing the light and shadow within us all."

"And what if that light flickers and dies?" Azazel's challenge rang through the clearing, but there was a tremor beneath his bravado this time. "What if chaos is the answer?"

"It isn't an answer—it's an evasion," Seraphiel responded with passion. "Can you not see that our true strength lies in our bonds? You call for chaos, but all it breeds is suffering. It is in our unity that we find the strength to overcome the darkness."

Liora turned her gaze to the others. Almost imperceptibly, heads nodded in agreement, the undercurrents of camaraderie starting to bind them. She felt a flicker of resilience igniting within the assembly. Here stood a multitude, each with their unique journeys, discovering connections that transcended their fears.

"What if…" Liora's voice soared now, catching the attention of every being present. "What if our alignment as allies holds the key to reclaiming the balance that has been lost? The prophecy speaks of choices and consequences, yes—but it is not written in stone."

A contemplative silence fell over the gathering, the weight of her words hanging in the stillness. Inspiration sparked in the eyes of those listening, a distant glimmer of possibility. If they were to make a stand, it would not be as isolated warriors but as a united front.

"And we will face our demons together," Ezekiel added resolutely, stepping beside her. "The impending cataclysm must not become our undoing. Our choices today will ripple through realms for eternity."

It was as if a wave of fervor washed over the crowd. Angels clasped hands with humans; fallen beings stood side by side with their celestial kin. It was an alliance born not of convenience, but of necessity—a kinship forged in the fires of impending conflict.

But doubt still lingered in the air, flickering like the shadows cast by the dying light of day. The Oracle perceived it too, her expression cryptic yet understanding. "Remember," she intoned softly. "Every decision you make is a thread in the tapestry of fate. The impending cataclysm may not merely be the end; it can also serve as a new beginning. What lies ahead is not beyond your control."

Liora absorbed that notion, reflecting on her own fears and desires. It was human to question, to fear the unknown—but perhaps within that uncertainty lay the seeds of change.

As evening descended, painting the horizon in hues of crimson and gold, Liora felt a sense of clarity blooming within her—a realization that their path was not among the shadows; it lay shrouded in the possibility of light. The impending cataclysm was not inevitable doom, but an invitation to become champions of their own futures.

"Then let us prepare," she declared, her heart thrumming with newfound purpose. "We must share our knowledge, our strengths. Let us train together and fortify our alliances as we brace for what is to come."

One by one, faces lit with determination as others echoed her sentiment. "Together," they asserted, a chorus of voices rising beneath the twilight sky.

The reality of their choices rushed toward them like a tidal wave, surging through their minds and hearts. They were faced not just with the question of how to combat the encroaching darkness, but with the irrevocable truth that unity was their greatest weapon.

As the gathering began to disperse, the last light of day glimmered with the promise of hope. Each character, each walking away, carrying their unique burdens, fears, and desires woven together in the shared tapestry of fate. They had come to grips with the gravity of the impending cataclysm, but now understood that it was their choice to confront it head-on, not as isolated individuals, but as a united front prepared to forge their destinies anew.

And as Liora stepped away from the clearing, her mind swirled with the echoes of the prophecy. It no longer felt like a shackle binding her to despair. Instead, it became a clarion call declaring the beauty of choice—the sacred power residing within each of them.

No matter what lay ahead, she was ready to stand with her allies against the darkness, determined to carve a path through uncertainty, for the world needed the glimmer of hope that they could provide, and Liora could embrace nothing less. Together, they would face the impending cataclysm, turning it into an opportunity for transformation—a chance to rewrite their destinies in the annals of time.

Gathering Forces

The moon hung low in the night sky, casting a silver glow upon the gathering beneath its light. Liora stood at the center of a clearing in the adjacent woods, her heart thrumming in rhythm with the feeling of urgency in the air. She sensed the tension between realms and the electricity of converging destinies.

Around her, figures clad in modest attire mingled; humans seeking strength in the shadows, their hope flickering like candles in a darkened room. They had arrived from scattered villages, drawn by whispers of a looming storm that threatened to tear the fabric of their reality apart.

Liora's gaze drifted over the small assembly. Each face held the stories of their struggles, their losses, and their unyielding desire to protect what remained of their world. "This is not just a fight for us," she began, her voice steady but laced with emotion, "but for our families, our children, our very way of life. I know you've all heard the tales—the angels, the fallen, and the monsters that now lurk at the edge of our realm, threatening all we hold dear."

A farmer stepped forward from the back of the gathering, his expression etched with doubt. "What can we do? We are mere mortals, armed with forks and plows. How can we stand against beings made of light and shadow?"

Liora felt the weight of his words, but she also felt the warmth of her own resolve. "You're right. We are not angels, but we are not powerless either. We have something that they do not—unity. Together, we can rally forces that even the mightiest of beings cannot ignore. Together, we can shine our light upon the encroaching darkness."

As murmurs of uncertainty began to rise, Ezekiel appeared within the clearing, his ethereal presence cutting through despair like a sharp blade through fog. The angel stood tall, wings whispering against the night air, radiating an iridescent glow that drew every eye. "Do not underestimate the power of humanity," he said, voice resonating like a bell of hope. "It is not the strength of arms that will win this battle. It is the strength of your hearts and your willingness to stand together, angels and humans alike. Trust in one another."

Liora felt emboldened; Ezekiel's reassurance wafted through her and ignited a spark of courage among the crowd. They were not mere mortals cowering before the divine; they were part of something far larger.

"For centuries, our realms have existed in parallel, bound by laws that few understand," Ezekiel continued, his gaze sweeping over the assemblage. "But now we must transcend those boundaries. We need to forge alliances with not just humans, but also the remaining angels who still believe in our shared purpose. We must wake them."

"What if they refuse to help us?" a voice called from the group. "What if the fallen angels—Azazel—turn against us?"

"They will not. Not all of them," Liora responded, her heart racing at the thought. "There are those among them who long for redemption, just as we wish to protect our homes." She locked eyes with Ezekiel, who nodded silently, affirming her determination. "I will seek out those who yearn for peace. I will speak with Seraphiel, the fallen who still clings to the remnants of his grace. We can start there."

The farmer clenched his fists, brows furrowing deeper. "And what do you suggest we do in the meantime? How do we prepare?"

Ezekiel stepped closer, wings folding as if to embrace them in a protective shroud. "We gather. We train. We strategize. In our meetings, we must weave together our strengths and our hopes. We must draw from every corner of the realm—reach out to the kin of the forgotten, call upon the spirits of the forest, the warriors of old. They will lend us their strength because they feel the pull of the impending battle like we do."

Liora looked at the faces surrounding her, many wounded by fear and doubt, but more emboldened by the presence of Ezekiel. "Let us each take a moment to remember why we are here. Each of you has faced darkness before. You have endured hardship and loss. Together, we can channel that pain into purpose. Let's transform our fear into courage."

Slowly, hands began to rise, voices beginning to chime in unison with her. Each whisper turned into another echo, forming an undercurrent of resolve. It was a ripple—first quiet, then gaining strength, finally crashing forth on waves of determination.

Hours swelled into days as they trained together, the humans learning from the ageless wisdom of their ethereal companions. Liora found herself invigorated, not only by the sight of valorous souls but also by the lessons brought forth from countless skirmishes, passed down through the generations. They practiced together in the early mornings as the first hints of daylight broke through the canopy and lingered late into the gloaming when their whispers melded into a single purpose.

In those moments, Liora and Ezekiel schemed. They established signals, coded messages woven into the movements of birds and rustling leaves. They traversed to nearby villages, serenading the hearts of the people with songs of unity, coaxing them to join their cause. They wrote letters, beseeching the remaining angels to meet in designated spots where barriers between their kinds could thin out, places where conversations could bloom and turn into coalitions.

And yet, doubt lingered within some corners of Liora's mind. During a quiet evening, she found herself wandering through a thicket of trees, seeking solace in the rustling leaves. The wind carried memories with it—the laughter of children, the cries of battle, and the whispers of long-forgotten promises.

As she walked, a slight figure emerged from behind the curtain of branches—a young demigod named Caelum. He possessed the look of his celestial heritage and the earnestness of humanity. "You're distressed," he said quietly, sensing the weight upon her shoulders.

"I am," Liora admitted, aware of how the young eyes watched her with heavy scrutiny. "The more we rally, the more I fear for what is to come. The fate we're weaving is fraught with uncertainty."

"Do you trust Ezekiel?" Caelum asked, tilting his head inquisitively.

"Yes, with everything I have," she replied.

"Then you must trust in your own strength as well," he implored, stepping closer. "We're all gathering for a common purpose, and I believe that the spirits are behind us. I feel it in my blood, Liora. You're the tether we need, the one to unite us all."

Liora pondered his words. He was young, but there was wisdom in his tone that had survived through the ages. She understood then; she was not alone in her doubts. This could be the moment they united against an unseen threat. "Let's gather the others at dawn," she resolved. "I want everyone here when I speak again."

As the first light broke over the horizon, hues of dawn kissed the treetops, and Liora appeared before the gathered souls once more. She could feel the energy hum within the air, the forgotten hope of alliances sparking to life at her fingertips. "Today, we face the possibility of our allies coming together for the first time," she announced, passion coursing through her. "This is our moment—our chance to reshape the narrative of our existence. We will not fight alone."

Liora felt power in unity, and she encouraged everyone in their pursuits. Warriors stepped forward, sharing their knowledge of battle strategy; farmers spoke of the land and weather, while artisans offered tools for improvisation. All people, celestial or human, contributed with genuine intent and ferocity that opened the doors of possibility.

As the day unfolded, tents of varying shapes and sizes sprang up around the clearing, creating a temporary haven filled with the hustle of activity. Humans set to work building defenses, crafting weapons, while the angels paired up with chosen mortals, becoming mentors in artful combat. Allies forged connections through shared burdens and the laughter that punctuated the tension in the air.

Trust began to blossom within this makeshift community—a living entity forged from disparate elements. As Liora traversed the encampment, she watched conversations unfold, friendships grow, and battles of ideas flourish into formations of righteousness.

But not everyone shared this brave resolve; whispers of dissent still lingered, especially among those unsure about the supposed unity between angels and humans. As she mingled with the crowd, Liora found herself approached by a group of fiery-eyed warriors who bore their anger openly.

"What are you doing?" one demanded, voice quaking with indignation. "These beings—these angels—what makes us think they'll fight for us? Our people have suffered too long beneath the shadows. How do we know they will not betray us again?"

"Betrayal walks alongside trust," Liora countered, her heart racing. "But this isn't a matter of blind faith. We're choosing to leap together into the unknown, rather than retreat within our shells! We must stand resolute against threats that prey upon division and fear. Every day asks us to reclaim our truths with every choice we make."

"What if it was our choice to go against them?" another voice challenged. "What if that is our only option left?"

At this, Liora's frustration flared. "Is conflict truly what you wish for? Are we not already suffering in silence beneath their shadows? This is the moment destiny presented us—a chance to unite! We'll only find true strength amid our vulnerability!"

Their expressions softened as they mulled over her words, the tension in the air shifting subtly. It would never be simple; she recognized that their fears were enslaved within her own vulnerability, raw and pulsing. But she also saw glimmers of hope sparkling amid those deep-set eyes.

As the sun dipped toward the horizon, casting amber and fiery hues across the landscape, messages carried by scouting birds fluttered into the camp. The time had come. Allies would arrive, not just from neighboring villages but from the abandoned realms of the divine. Liora felt the tightening grip of destiny, knowing that their stand would soon unfold.

She stood on a makeshift podium at the heart of the clearing, her blood pounding, adrenaline coursing through her veins as she prepared to address the crowd. "Hear me, friends!" Her voice echoed, gripping each ear with fervor. "Tonight, we join together not only as humans but as those who trust in the celestial remaining threads that bind us! Let this night serve as a beacon for our allies! If we stand united, we can breathe life into the prophecy that binds our fates!"

All at once, lights twinkled in the distance—a gathering of figures emerged from the veil of the treeline. A hush descended over the gathering as they beheld the angels, their ethereal forms glimmering like starlight against the encroaching darkness. Among them stood Seraphiel, his silhouette a shadow of glorious resilience draped in golden light.

Liora gasped. The moment she had been praying for had arrived—but so too had the reality that this alliance could harbor the greatest potential for both salvation and ruin.

The meeting of realms began, hope clashing with uncertainty on the brink of crisis. As they stepped forward to embrace their predestined destiny, Liora steeled herself, knowing full well the impending storm would test every bond they had forged together.

With united breaths, they prepared to march against their fates, hearts ablaze with the fire of their shared purpose. Let them come; for within the walls of their thrown-together community, Liora felt a powerful truth awakening—together, they were warriors upon the precipice of a new dawn, armed with more than weapons but the very essence of their souls daring to defy the darkness.

8

The Choice of Humanity

Moral Dilemmas

In the dim light of the gathering storm, the air crackled with tension as the reality of their situation settled heavily upon the shoulders of humanity. News of the celestial battles along the veil had spread like wildfire, igniting fears and anxieties that had long lain dormant within the hearts of the people. Liora stood at the heart of this chaos, feeling the weight of uncountable eyes turned toward her for answers she did not possess. The revelations about angels and monsters had torn through their lives, shattering the comforting illusions they clung to. And now, standing amidst the shuddering remains of faith and fear, humanity faced a defining choice—a choice that hinged upon the very essence of belief, morality, and survival.

Two streets converged near the outskirts of her village: one that led to the sacred grove and the ancient altar, where prayers had been offered for generations, and the other into the heart of the city, where doubt and despair echoed through the cracks in the cobblestones. In days past, the path toward the grove had been a singular expression of devotion, a well-worn way of life where faith flourished in the embrace of bright beliefs. Today, as Liora looked at both roads, they seemed to bifurcate not just in direction but in the very notions of existence and reality that governed their lives.

Gatherings of villagers had formed; their faces etched with worry and uncertainty. Some hoisted pitchforks and lanterns, rallying to defend their homes against the invisible chaos that lurked just beyond their understanding. Conversely, others sought solace in prayer, attempting to invoke whatever divine forces could be summoned to protect their existence. But as the debates raged, the pressing question emerged: What did it mean to trust in the divine after witnessing the horrors that came from the celestial realms? Were their guardian angels truly just that, or were they just as capable of malevolence?

In the midst of her fear and uncertainty, Liora found herself unexpectedly called to address the people. Stepping onto the makeshift platform, her heart raced, and a chorus of murmurs ebbed and flowed like an ever-present tide. She felt the expectant sigh of the crowd washing over her, a collective hope mixed with doubt. How could she rally a people fragmented by the very ideologies that were meant to unite them?

"We can no longer hide from the truth," Liora began, her voice steady despite the tremor lurking within. "We have witnessed the darkness that exists beyond our realm—the battles between angels and monsters. It is easy to see only what is before us—the monster willing to prey upon our fears—but we must not forget the legacies left by the angels, either. They were sent to protect us, yet their fall reminds us that power is a double-edged sword. We stand at the precipice of a choice. We must decide: do we hold fast to our beliefs, embrace the divine, and stand alongside our celestial protectors? Or do we cast aside our faith and, in so doing, lose ourselves to the darkness that seeks to consume us?"

She could see doubts etched on the faces before her, the flickering candles illuminating eyes that reflected faith, fear, and unshed tears. In this pivotal moment, she understood the magnitude of their moral dilemma. Each soul pondered the fragility of their existence and the weight of belief—how easily it could tip from hope to despair. What had once been simple devotion became a kaleidoscope of perspectives, revealing the vast layers of human experience.

While Liora addressed the crowd, a voice rang out from the back. It belonged to a man Liora recognized as Elias, a former carpenter turned blacksmith, whose hands bore the scars of a hard life and deep wisdom. "You speak of angels, but do we not live with the monsters among us?" he questioned, his voice firm yet edged with the tremor of vulnerability. "How many of us have lost loved ones to the chaos that the fallen created? How can we trust those who have strayed from the light? Are we to embrace the very beings who watched, who did nothing, as evil took root in this world?"

The murmurs rose again as people considered Elias's words, their doubts ignited like kindling caught in flame. Liora knew that he articulated a truth rooted in pain, real, tangible loss that resonated painfully with every heart that beat among them. It was a crucial point, illuminating the chasm that separated their experiences from a faith that felt abstracted and distant.

But what could she say in response? How could she overshadow the reality that monsters existed, both within and outside of their realm? Each family had a story, woven out of love and loss, a reminder of how chaos crept into their realities. Some had lost children, parents, and siblings to battles that had spilled over from the celestial planes. For many, faith had become bitter, souring their hearts against the divine.

Yet amidst despair came the memories of light, the tender moments of protection and hope forged by angelic hands. Liora recalled the times when dreams brought forth solace, whispers of guidance that steered her through trials. And perhaps, just perhaps, the divine still held a role to play.

"We must recognize the duality within every being—every angel and every monster," she pressed on, drawing from the depths of her own experience. Her voice bore the echoes of inner conviction, trembling yet rising to meet the hearts that had grown weary. "Fallen beings remind us of the dangers of unchecked power, while angels who remain resolute in their faith demand our loyalty in the face of adversity. It is not faith itself that is flawed, but rather how we wield it. Each of us must decide for ourselves whether to amplify the good or succumb to the darkness."

Slowly, the crowd began to respond, soft murmurs rising in acknowledgment, unsure yet inquisitive about the path forward. Moral dilemmas had a tendency to yield a spectrum of human experience. Liora could feel the weight of their uncertainty pressing against her, wrapping her words in hesitation that teetered on the edge of reason.

Meanwhile, in far corners of the gathering, other voices arose, echoing different concerns. Young Aveline—no more than fifteen, with fiery red hair and dreams of adventure—stood up beside her mother. "I want to believe in the angels," she said, her voice trembling yet fierce. "But what if we are only being used? What if they take more than they give? How much more suffering must we endure before they decide to help us?"

From currents of hesitation, more voices joined in—a swell of unease that threatened to drown out any notions of belief. Each soul brought their doubts to the surface, reflecting Liora's own quandary. The desire to trust in angels might be a privilege, but did it erase their agony? As time pressed on, the worries of the human heart assumed many forms: indignation, skepticism, longing, and heartbreak.

"We all suffer," Liora reiterated, her spirit igniting against the encroaching shadows. "And yes, we've seen our world turned upside down. But I urge you to reflect on our decisions as a function of who we trust and what kind of people we want to become. If we give in to distrust and abandon faith entirely, we risk becoming the very monsters we fear. Resentment will breed only more suffering."

The path forward was riddled with challenges, and Liora knew she had to guide them through these moral complexities. As she stood before them, she considered her relationship with Ezekiel, the guardian angel who had witnessed her struggles and celebrated her victories. While her faith in him remained unshaken, she felt the dissonance of others echoing around her. Others might question their angels' loyalty or grapple with their own pain. Could she rally strength from the heavens despite uncertainty permeating the mortal world?

In that moment of introspection, a flicker of hope ignited within—a reminder that the angels, too, were bound by their own battles with grace and gravity. They grappled with identities altered by choices, longing for reconciliation and redemption. After all, it was the essence of humanity that pulled them together—that intrinsic bond that tied soul to soul, transcending the tumultuous divide. Maybe this struggle for belief represented the eternal push-pull that stitched reality together in all its brutal beauty.

And so, Liora gathered her resolve. She continued to speak, her words more impassioned. "In this moment of crisis, we are called to define ourselves—not merely as victims of a world turned upside down but as champions of our moral landscape. We have a choice. We can pick up arms and strike against the darkness, allowing desperation to erode the fabric of our humanity, or we can rise and empower ourselves to find common ground. We can choose to stand for peace, embrace uncertainty, and still believe love has the power to overcome even the deepest stains of betrayal."

The crowd shifted, a palpable energy filling the air, laden with uncertainty yet sprinkled with deep yearning. Each voice began to contribute to the chorus, distilling their own fears and hopes into a collective awareness. It seeped into the very core of their beings, prompting reflection far deeper than the impending struggle against external forces. The philosophical discourse revealing itself amidst the turmoil epitomized the reality of their humanity—the beautiful, messy, and infinitely complex experience they all shared.

In the heart of everything—the love and ache, the hope and despair, the reverence clashing with the visceral instinct for survival—Liora realized they were partaking in a delicate dance of decisions. It stirred beautifully within the folds of their consciousness, navigating the storms of faith and doubt. Would they hold onto the threads of belief that tethered them to their celestial progenitors, or would the lure of chaos convince them to sever those ties and embrace a different path?

The unfolding conversation touched upon the dual nature of their plight as they acknowledged the warm light of purpose often dimmed by the chilling grip of existential fear. Smiles emerged among the anxious faces like embers igniting, and Liora felt hope surge within the thrumming pulse of her own heart—a reminder that despite the trials they faced, the human spirit never wavered.

As her address reached its climax, Liora took a breath. "Let us choose belief, not blindly, but as a testament to our resilience. We will weather the storm together. We will summon our courage to confront the monsters that seek to devour us, not just the ones who dwell in the shadows, but the inner turmoil that tests our very essence. May our hearts be forged anew amid the pain and suffering, born from the knowledge that we reclaim our narratives through love, understanding, and unity."

Around her, whispers morphed into a developing resolve, a gathering affirmation that the collective force of their beliefs could bridge the chasm often bridged by chaos. Answers might still elude them, clarity hidden behind layers of suffering and uncertainty, but together they shimmied against despair—their struggles forming an intricate tapestry that spoke of their humanity.

With connection forged through shared vulnerability, losses weighed against hope became the cornerstone of their decision. They would stare into the abyss not with dread but with the recognition of the countless hands in their hearts guiding their steps. Together, they would choose their path forward amid the impending cataclysm of uncertainty.

The Gathering Storm

The air hung heavy with an impending sense of doom. Dark clouds gathered ominously in the sky, swirling like a tempest poised to spill its fury upon the world below. Once vibrant and thriving, the landscape bore the scars of conflict, and the smell of earth dampened by rain mingled with the anticipation of chaos. Humanity was on the brink, caught between the forces of light and shadow, and Liora stood in the eye of this gathering storm, grappling with the weight of her destiny.

In the silence before the tempest, the whispers of the divine echoed in her mind—visions of angels soaring high above the clouds, their luminescence piercing the dark veil that loomed over their realm. But among them, she saw figures twisted and contorted by resentment and longing, embodying the very monsters they once fought against. Liora felt the pulse of these emotions beneath her skin, a relentless reminder of the choices that loomed ahead.

"Liora!" a voice pierced the darkness, shattering her reverie. It was Micah; his expression was a mixture of concern and determination. "We need to move. They're gathering at the bluff."

The urgency in Micah's voice drew her back to the present, where the reality of their impending confrontation settled like a stone in her gut. The once-familiar sense of purpose had morphed into something heavier, an expectation that felt suffocating. She rose to her feet, brushing the dirt from her skirt as she took a deep breath, steeling herself to confront the fear clawing at her heart.

"Right," she replied, keeping her voice steady despite the tremor in her hands. "Let's go."

The journey to the bluff was fraught with tension. Each step was a reminder of the stakes: the lives of her loved ones, the fate of those who could not defend themselves, and the dwindling hope that a peaceful resolution was still possible. The world around them reflected their inner turmoil; the trees swayed violently as a gust of wind whipped through, branches scraping against one another like the sound of clashing swords.

Micah cast her sidelong glances, sensing the storm within her. "You're quiet. What's going on in that head of yours?"

Liora hesitated. "I just—what if we lose? What if all this fighting leads to nothing?" Her voice cracked slightly, vulnerability seeping through her facade of strength. She had wrestled with questions like these in her mind, contorting her thoughts until they were almost unrecognizable, but sharing them felt different. It was terrifyingly real.

"Every battle comes with risks," Micah said, his tone steady. "But if we don't fight—if we don't stand up for what we believe in—we've already lost."

She wanted to believe him, but doubt clung to her like a shadow. The enormity of her choices loomed larger than ever, and the fear of failure threatened to drown her resolve. She had been gifted with visions, but those gifts felt like chains now, binding her to a path she was unsure she could walk. Beyond the predictive glimpses of the future lay a chasm of uncertainty, threatening to swallow her whole.

As they approached the bluff, the atmosphere thickened, charged with an electricity that tingled on Liora's skin. She could hear the distant roar of voices, the rising tension of souls preparing for battle. The ragtag assembly of humans, a mix of seasoned fighters and untrained civilians, stood at the precipice. They shared glances filled with trepidation and determination, warriors in the midst of a brewing storm.

"Listen up!" a commanding voice boomed through the crowd—it was Ezekiel, the archangel. His presence filled the space around him like a beacon of light against the swelling darkness. "The time has come for us to confront the threat beyond our world. We stand together, not just for ourselves but for everything we hold dear!"

Cheers erupted from the crowd, resonating with a shared defiance against the chaos lying in wait. Liora watched Ezekiel, her heart racing. Here was a being forged in the fires of heaven, commanding strength and unwavering resolve. And yet, in the archangel's eyes, she detected a flicker of concern—an acknowledgment of vulnerabilities that she could relate to. He was not immune to fear, just as she was not immune to the weight of her own choices.

"Are you ready to fight?" Micah's voice snapped her back to him, piercing through the fog of her thoughts.

Liora opened her mouth to respond, but the truth clawed at her throat. This was more than just a war; this was a culmination of choices—some made for her, others she had to seize. She had felt the weight of countless destinies rest upon her shoulders, and as the clouds grew darker, it seemed her own heart echoed the tempest brewing above.

"I don't know if I am," she finally admitted, her breath shallow. "What if I make the wrong choice?"

"Every choice comes with its doubts," Micah said, his voice firm yet gentle. "But none of us can unravel the threads of power that bind us. The only way to move forward is to embrace that uncertainty."

His conviction sparked something within her. Perhaps it was enough to hold onto an ember of courage amidst the escalating storm. Her life had been intertwined with angels and monsters; she had glimpsed the threads of fate weave through her existence. Now, it was time to confront it head-on.

Liora took a deep breath, her resolve shaping into determination as she stepped toward the gathering crowd, heart racing but mind clear. "Listen!" she called out, her voice rising above the murmurs. The crowd hushed, their eyes turning toward her. "We may feel fear, doubt, and uncertainty—but we are not alone. We are bound by our choices, and we can create our destiny together!"

Ezekiel's gaze met hers, an approving nod encouraging her burgeoning spirit. Micah stood behind her, his energy radiating support. She felt a warmth swell within, igniting an unquenchable fire.

"The forces against us are powerful," Liora continued, her voice gaining strength. "But we have something they cannot take away from us—our unity! Our love for one another! Together, we can face them! We can challenge the darkness and hopefully find compassion even in the heart of despair!"

As she spoke, determination surged through the gathered souls like a wave, building excitement and solidarity among them. Faces she recognized—friends, neighbors, strangers—each revealed a flicker of hope in the depths of their eyes. It reminded her that they were not merely fighting for survival; they were fighting for everything worth living for.

The atmosphere shifted, bolstered by the fire of their collective spirit. It swept over the crowd, uniting them in purpose. With that surge of energy came a newfound urgency—each heartbeat resonated an unspoken agreement among them, fueling their resolve. They were no longer individuals caught in their doubts, but a collective force capable of shifting the very balance of power.

A distant rumble of thunder echoed like a war drum, reminding them of the storm yet to come. And yet, Liora felt an exhilarating clarity settle over her. This storm, both inside and out, was a crucible wherein their strength would be forged. Fear was inevitable, but it would no longer dictate their actions.

"Let's move!" Ezekiel's booming voice broke through the haze, his wings unfurling as radiance exploded around him. "We fight not just for ourselves, but for every soul that dreams of a brighter future! We march into the storm!"

With those words, an electric charge surged through the crowd, mirroring the brewing tempest in the heavens. Liora felt it blaze through her veins, and she raised her chin higher, ready to embrace the challenge ahead. As they marched forward to meet the forces of darkness, determination coursed from the ground beneath her feet all the way to the skies above.

It was time.

With a battle cry that resonated through the air, Liora and her companions surged forward, confronting the darkness that loomed ahead. The sound of pounding feet and fierce cries melded with the thunder, igniting an undeniable symphony of defiance echoing against the storm's fury.

But as they moved toward the precipice of conflict, Liora's mind remained haunted by the echoes of possibility—the choices yet to be made, the lives yet to be saved or lost. Each step ignited a resolve within her, granting her the courage to stand against the encroaching shadows that threatened to engulf everything she held dear.

The storm was rising, both within and above, but Liora knew one thing above all: she was ready to confront whatever awaited them just beyond the horizon. It was not just a battle for survival; it was a choice to reclaim their future, to reforge the ties that bound them together, and to embrace the uncertainty that lay ahead. Their voices rang out, a collective rallying cry against the darkness as they plunged into the storm, ready to meet the challenge with hearts ablaze.

And so, as the skies ruptured into chaos, Liora felt an ember ignite within her—a promise of resilience, of courage, and of the unyielding spirit of humanity that could weather any storm.

The Choice

The sun hung low over the horizon, casting long shadows across the once-vibrant town square. The air was thick with an unshakable tension, an electric buzz that seemed to vibrate through the very soil beneath their feet. The chaos of the recent battles—fiery clashes between fallen angels, monsters, and humanity—had left their mark. Crumbled buildings and scattered remnants of a life once lived painted a haunting backdrop to the gathering crowd.

At the center of it all stood Liora, gripping a crude wooden staff that had served as her only weapon in the perilous journey leading to this moment. Her heart raced with a mixture of fear and determination as she looked out at her fellow townspeople. They had come together in the face of despair, united by a thread of hope that pulsed through the air like the faintest whisper of the divine. Beneath her tough exterior lay the weight of an impossible decision looming on the horizon—one that could alter the courses of their lives forever.

Around her, faces mirrored her anxiety. The mayor, a once-stalwart leader now etched with lines of worry and uncertainty, stepped forward, his voice trembling yet resolute. "We have lost much, and many of us still bear visible and hidden scars. We stand at the precipice of choice today, with the fates of our families, our town, and our very souls weighing on our shoulders. Do we forge ahead into the uncertainty, or do we turn back to the safety of ignorance?"

Liora felt the gravity of his words, resonating deep within her. She had witnessed the horrors unleashed by Azazel and his monstrous allies and recalled the visions—the divine messages that had guided her thus far. Yet, intertwined with those visions was a reluctant truth: they had been as much a curse as they were a blessing. The uncertainty of sacrifice loomed larger than ever, and she wondered if she could bear the weight of another loss.

"We must face the reality of our situation," Liora called out, her voice steady despite the churning anxiety within her. "We have seen the darkness, felt its cold grip around our hearts. But we also possess the power to rise up together. This choice is our ultimate test of resilience and unity. We are not alone; we have each other and the potential to choose our own fate."

A murmur of agreement rippled through the crowd as her words seemed to stir a spark of hope. Yet, doubt lingered in the air, like an insistent fog. Among the crowd stood members of the town's council, their expressions betraying the conflicts that danced behind closed doors. One elder, a man revered for his wisdom, stepped forward, shaking his head gently. "But Liora, to embrace this fight means to invite chaos into our midst. How can we trust in the promises of those who wield such power? What if we place our faith in the wrong hands?"

The tension in the square thickened. Liora's heart sank as she watched familiar faces shift uneasily. It was a valid point, and the fear that often accompanied uncertainty was palpable. How could they put their trust in unseen forces, be they angelic or otherwise, when darkness had already seeped into their lives?

"Because inaction will only lead us to ruin," Liora shot back, her fervor igniting her voice. "We cannot stand idle while Azazel's forces prey upon us. I have witnessed their brutality. If we do not fight back, we risk losing everything we hold dear. The monsters know no mercy. We must choose between enduring this torment or rising to meet it. What would you have us do? Hide in the shadows like frightened children while the world crumbles around us?"

Every eye in the square bore into her, weighing her words against the heavy anchor of fear. She could feel their conflicting emotions, the stifling grip of dread against the flickering ember of hope. It was in this crucible of emotion that Liora's determination hardened. They were standing at a crossroads, one where the lines between right and wrong blurred and the complexities of morality warped under the weight of survival.

Ezekiel, the angel who had guided and protected her, floated above the crowd, his presence a stark reminder of the thin veil that separated them from the realms beyond. His voice, soothing yet commanding, resonated through the air. "You wander in a world filled with shadows, but it is within you to ignite the light. You must trust in yourselves, for only you can forge the path forward together. Embrace faith in each other; within that bond lies your strength."

The weight of his words struck deep. Liora shifted her gaze to the faces around her, and she saw more than fear; she saw resilience beginning to flicker to life. She took another breath, seeking to reassure them. "Each one of you has already made sacrifices. Those sacrifices have woven us together in ways we cannot fully comprehend. Trust in that bond. Trust in our shared humanity, the very essence that makes us who we are."

Voices began to rise amongst the crowd, supporting her words. It was as if a dormant spirit had awakened within them—a yearning for change, a desire for freedom from the shackles of fear that had long paralyzed them.

Wooden faces became softened; the council members exchanged glances filled with newfound resolve. An elderly woman, her hands trembling yet fierce, stepped forward. "We have suffered too long to let fear dictate our lives. I choose to fight for my grandchildren—for their future. I choose us."

A ripple of agreement surged through the crowd. "I choose to fight!" another voice cried, a young man barely out of his teens raising a fist, eyes shining with feverish determination.

The townspeople began to chant, a chorus of unwavering voices rising as each chose faith over fear, hope over uncertainty. Liora felt her own spirit lift alongside theirs, the tide of their collective determination washing over her like a cleansing wave. In that moment, they were no longer mere townsfolk; they were a people reborn, a united front against the creeping shadows that sought to consume them.

As their rallying call reached its peak, Liora realized that their collective choice was not merely to fight against the darkness but to embrace the light within themselves. They chose to believe that even in the face of chaos, even surrounded by monsters, they had the capacity to challenge the very fabric of good and evil.

But even as hope surged, a familiar chill caused an involuntary shiver to run down her spine. Beneath this newfound courage lay a raw, unsteady fear — what if they failed? What if the forces they faced were far more insurmountable than they ever imagined? It was a spiritual gamble, one that posed the risk of unimaginable loss.

Then, the ground trembled, a warning tremor felt even from the heights of Ezekiel's ethereal form. The air turned heavy, laden with a foreboding presence. "They've come," he declared, his voice grave and commanding.

Murmurs rolled through the crowd like distant thunder as unease crept back in. Palpable and suffocating darkness began to envelop the town, swirling ominously around them like a ravenous predator. The townsfolk turned their heads, eyes widening as shadowy figures descended upon the edges of the town square.

Liora's heart raced. This was it, the moment she had prepared for yet feared with all her being. But now, with the collective decision made, they would not face this invasion alone. She looked out into the resolute faces of her fellow townspeople. There was no turning back.

"We stand together!" she called, raising her staff high alongside the gathering clouds, a symbol of their unity. "We will not be cowed by fear!

We choose to fight for our future!"

The echo of her voice heralded a resounding cheer from the crowd. They were ready to defend their home, to protect their kin.

Ezekiel surveyed the newcomers, and his resolution was clear. "Fight with conviction, for you are not just warriors; you are the embodiment of hope against despair."

As the first of the shadowy figures emerged from the dark, grotesque forms twisting and writhing before them, Liora felt something shift within her. Each breath steadied her resolve; she had chosen not only to fight but to embrace the chaos, to be a part of something far greater than herself.

Yet, as the monsters approached, something deep within her began to stir—a reminder of the cost of such choices. Whispers of doubt echoed, warnings of betrayal and sacrifice danced just out of reach. How many lives would the choice to fight cost? And what would the price be for the lives they sought to protect?

The air intensified, a thick tension wrapping around her as shadows melded with the figures of the monstrous horde. She would have to confront her own fears while leading her people into the heart of chaos.

The first monstrous figure drew closer—a sprawling mass that resembled nightmares shaped from shadows, twisting upon itself in a ghastly form. Liora could see teeth glistening, ready to devour. Her heart thundered against her ribs, a reminder of her humanity amidst the surreal threat. She tightened her grip around her staff, steeling her nerves.

"It's time, Liora," Ezekiel urged, hovering beside her like a guardian poised to protect. "What choice will you make now? Will you stand and fight, or will you give in to fear?"

Liora's heart surged, igniting with clarity. She took a step forward, rallying strength from the souls around her. "We choose to fight together!" she shouted with conviction, her voice rising above the crescendo of approaching chaos.

In that moment of collective will, she felt the oppressive weight of uncertainty begin to lift. Humanity's choice stretched out before them—a harbinger of connection and courage that soared above the monstrous forms advancing.

The clash was inevitable; the battle for their future was beginning.

Yet, just as they prepared to unleash their defiance, the ground shook with renewed fervor, sending shock waves through the square. From the darkness emerged a majestic silhouette, towering above the chaos—a figure cloaked in radiant light that interrupted the encroaching shadows.

A voice boomed, reverberating against the very foundations of the world itself, "You stand united, uncertain yet strong. What will you do when darkness tests your resolve?"

Liora's breath caught, her heart racing against the unexpected presence. It was one of the most powerful intrigues—an angel among them, a figure that demanded answers.

"Together!" she shouted with conviction. "We will fight!"

As the angel's glow enveloped them, a breathtaking moment of clarity pierced through the chaos, leaving them suspended between light and shadow. The air crackled with energy, an intensity of choice and consequence as they steeled themselves for the coming storm.

Liora peered into the faces surrounding her, and in that moment, she realized the truth—whatever awaited them would only strengthen their bonds and remind them of why they had chosen to fight.

The question hung heavy in the air, echoing as time stood still—what choice would they make as one, in the face of the encroaching darkness?

As the forces of light and shadow converged, the path forward remained steeped in uncertainty. But amidst the fear and doubt, hope forged its way through the labyrinth of choices laid ahead. The real battleground had shifted from external conflict to an urgent reckoning within the hearts of humanity.

With that newfound strength tethered by unity, Liora raised her voice alongside the call of her people, ready to confront the shadows that threatened to swallow them whole.

And as the clash began, the suffocating tension balanced on the precipice of a cliffhanger, leaving them suspended between their fate and the choices still unraveling, teetering on the brink of all they held so dearly.

9

Reconciliation or Ruin

The Clash of Realms

The air was thick with tension, crackling like the surface of the sun, as the three realms prepared for their clash. The winds howled a frantic symphony, echoing the chaos of celestial warfare that was about to unfold. Humanity, caught in the crossfire, stood at the precipice of annihilation or salvation; their courage teetered on a knife's edge against the onslaught of darkness.

At the heart of it all, Seraphiel soared high above the battlefield, his once-pristine wings now streaming with the dust of his fallen kin. Below him, the earth trembled as legions of monsters encroached, their forms grotesque and nightmarish. He could see Azazel's banner unfurling in the distance, a dark flag that billowed like a storm cloud heralding ruin. The fallen angel's laughter rang out, full of malice and delight, a sound that clawed at Seraphiel's heart.

"Are you ready to embrace your doom, brother?" Azazel taunted, voice carried by the wind, twisted with echoes of their once-brotherly bond. "Or will you simply succumb to your own nobility?"

The weight of Seraphiel's duty pressed heavily upon him. He had spent centuries guarding humanity, watching them grow, suffer, and rise again from the ashes of despair. But now, with humanity's existence hanging by a thread, he felt the burden of their collective hope. If he were to prevail, he would need to channel their determination—their intrinsic will to fight back against a formidable darkness which, until now, had seemed invincible.

Elsewhere in the skies, Liora prepared to join the fight. The visions she had received echoed in her mind: images of devastation entwined with whispers of hope. She had come to understand her role in this conflict, not merely as a passive observer but as a beacon of courage for those who believed. Her heart raced as she mounted her steed, a remarkable creature born of both worlds, glimmering with celestial energy and draped in shadows. The whispers of the divine surged through her, filling her with conviction and purpose. She was woven into the very fabric of this clash, and through her, humanity's indomitable spirit could blaze brightly.

With a rallying cry, Liora descended into the fray, her heart steeled by the resonant echoes of her purpose. The ground moved beneath her as warriors from both realms clashed. Every strike peeled back layers of fear, revealing resilience she had never known she possessed, just as it peeled back the bravado of Azazel's twisted ambition. She struck down a monstrous figure, the blade glinting in the fading twilight, and tasted the metallic tang of battle on her lips.

On the ground, chaos reigned. Beings of beauty and light clashed with grotesque fiends from the abyss, war cries blending with the belching roars of monsters. Seraphiel plummeted from above, engaging in the fray. His sword gleamed with divine light, illuminating the darkness that seemed to envelop every inch of the earth.

"Fight for them! Fight for everyone!" he shouted, projecting his voice into the hearts of the warriors. They responded with a roar, courage swelling within them, as if the very essence of his spirit poured into their veins. They charged forward, a tide of humanity swarming to take back their future.

Azazel was everywhere, a dark comet who danced through the smoke and gore of the battlefield. With every swipe of his ebony blade, he unleashed chaos, cutting through human and angel alike. He reveled in the destruction, a fiend in his element; he drew strength from the mayhem and shrouded warriors in shadows, rallying them with promises of power and freedom from divine constraint.

"Do you see it, Seraphiel? This is what the universe truly craves! The balance of power skewed toward chaos, where one can carve their legacy in blood," Azazel beckoned, drawing forth a cacophony of monsters. "Your angelic rules are nothing but shackles! We can shatter them all, join us!"

Seraphiel's heart surged with both fury and sorrow. His brother stood before him, not as the angel he once knew, but as a twisted reflection of what their bond had become. The rage within him ignited, but beneath that fire lurked the shadow of pity. He had witnessed Azazel's descent into madness, the rebellion that had ripped apart their kinship. How could one who had soared with the seraphim once now embody such hatred?

But there was no time left for hesitation. The moment's reality rushed forward as a wave crested in the sea; he ground his teeth deep into his resolve and battled forward. For every fallen angel who had lost their way, he was their only hope. For every child bringing hope to the world's darkness, he would not falter.

The clash of blades erupted around him, angels and warriors struggling for balance in the chaos. Liora emerged in a flurry, surrounded by vivid bursts of light as she fought valiantly alongside others. Seraphiel's heart swelled with pride as he witnessed humanity rising against the shadows. Their willingness to fight for a life worth living was the very essence that could tilt the battle.

"Together!" Liora shouted as she cleaved through a grotesque form, eyes raging with fire. "Stay united! We are stronger than they would have us believe!"

Hope stirred with every word she issued, like lifeblood coursing into every soul fighting around her. The humans rallied by her side, determination igniting them once again as they pushed back against the tide of darkness.

Yet, as the skirmish escalated, the deeper conflict surged within Seraphiel. He launched into the air, where he could see the battlefield as a whole—a grand tapestry marred by the horrors of war. Every strike he made resonated within him, each clash of steel sending ripples through his very core. As he battled Azazel, each blow reverberated with regrets, memories of laughter and light intertwined with the screams and cries for salvation.

"Brother," he uttered as they faced each other amidst the chaos, a fragile bond hanging by threads woven from the past. "Why have you let this darkness consume you? Remember who we were! What can we be? You don't have to continue down this path!"

A flicker ignited within Azazel's gaze, a brief return to the angel who had once soared by his side. But then, the shadows reasserted their hold, and he sneered, his voice low and bitter. "You cling to your naive hope while the world shatters around you. You think I can return? Redemption is a lie fabricated by our creators to keep us trapped in their design. We will reshape existence!"

Seraphiel could feel every ounce of anger coursing through Azazel, every shattering betrayal as they clashed with renewed intensity. It weighed on him, not merely as a foe before him, but as a tragic remnant of a soul once bright.

Meanwhile, Liora battled fiercely, each encounter forging unity between angels and humans. She watched as they pushed back against the relentless tide of darkness. Her heart pounded as hope surged and swelled, vowing to fight alongside Seraphiel—betwixt angel and man, embodying a bridge that could transform their intertwined fates.

Just as she felt invincible, another wave of monsters surged through the ranks, throwing both sides into disarray. A monstrous figure loomed ahead, and she gasped, recognizing the form, brimming with the malice of hunger and chaos. The beasts roared and faltered, their cries blending in a discordant symphony of desperation.

Yet, in the most critical moment, with terror clawing deep, Liora conjured her strength, beckoning forth her visions. The echoes of destiny cascaded around her, guiding her swiftly. She charged at the horde with renewed vigor, her blade slicing through darkness, cutting away the despair lingering in the air.

"Hold your ground!" she yelled, rallying those who faltered. "Together, we stand as one! Fear must not conquer our hearts!"

Her words reached into the thick of combat, igniting reason amidst the frenzy. The warriors around her rallied, humanity's unyielding spirit buckling against the encroaching chaos.

But just at that moment, Azazel unleashed a surge of sheer power, a dark whirlwind filled with regret and fury, aimed directly at Seraphiel. Time slowed as Seraphiel dodged, feeling the wind rip past him like a gentle whisper of death. Yet even in the chaos, there lay a shadow of redemption. He mirrored Azazel's movements, reaching out toward his brother, feeling the pull of their bond through their shared choices.

"For the love of all that is holy, do not let the darkness consume you!" he cried, his own voice drowning in the echoes of their past. "Together, we can bring back the light! It's not too late!"

Their blades locked, a flash of light igniting in the darkness, threatening to fracture the world. Azazel's mouth twisted in rage, yet there was a glimmer of indecision in his eyes. Seraphiel pressed into the moment, sharing the breath of their shared history—the laughter, camaraderie, and light they once embraced.

"The choice is yours, Azazel!" Seraphiel shouted, each word laced with desperation. "Choose yourself, or choose the darkness! The conflict you seek only leads to ruin! Redemption may still lie ahead!"

With every word, Liora's voice melded into their fates, intertwining amid the ruin of their battlefield, echoing along the choices they had to embrace. Just beyond, she witnessed their collision, feeling the tremor of choice ripple through the very air, a desperate call for unity amidst the chaos.

A moment hung, fragile and fraught, where the battle seemed to pause. Azazel recoiled, uncertainty pulsing through him like a heartbeat echoing both desire and fear. Seraphiel sensed it; the fleeting shadow of hope flickered behind Azazel's gaze, sparking a choice yet unmade.

Then fate intervened. The roster of chaos cracked open again as a horde descended upon them. Monsters surged forward like a dark tide, threatening to obscure every emerging glimmer of hope. Seraphiel and Azazel, locked in their brotherly struggle, turned their attention back to the battlefield as humanity rallied under Liora's captaincy.

With the fate of realms poised on the edge of a blade, Liora rallied her strength, knowing that unity was the only path capable of breaking the chains of despair. She propelled herself into the fray, determined to embrace her destiny and use it as a shield against the encroaching darkness.

"Now, we fight!" she shouted, her voice a clarion call against the roar of destruction. It echoed over the tumult, illuminating all that lay beneath the shadow of chaos.

The time for decision loomed, a critical moment destined to alter the very fabric of reality, threatening the balance of power itself. With each character faced with their inner turmoil amidst the battle, memories flashed—each defining choice, each heart laid bare under the fury of war. Would they succumb to ruin, allowing darkness to claim them, or could there be a turning tide toward reconciliation?

Time held its breath, each warrior poised for war yet yearning for unity. And as they faced the impending storm, they stood at the precipice of choice—a crossroads in existence where humanity would become the arbiter of future possibilities, shaping realms anew.

In this moment, bold and desperate, the culmination of the clash poured forth, forcing humanity to reckon with its demons, angels with their faith, and Azazel with the fragments of his own shattered being. The battle raged on, yet within that immense chaos, hope throbbed like a pulse. Love and sacrifice forged anew could shape destiny, squeezing life into the fractures of despair. What choices would echo into eternity?

Little did they know that the choices made tonight would resound across realms, threading the fate written in the stars. As the last gleam of twilight fell, the battle surged, and the fates of angels, monsters, and humanity hung precariously. Tomorrow would arrive, and within its light, choices would condemn or redeem them all.

The Aftermath

The battle had left an imprint on the landscape that neither humans nor celestial beings could ignore. The aftermath lay like a shroud over the world, heavy with silence, punctuated only by the distant echoes of what once was. Once vibrant fields became scarred wastelands, and the heavens, once a shimmering expanse of blue and gold, bore the traces of darkened shadows, reminiscent of the fierce confrontation that had unfolded.

As dawn broke, it unveiled a world altered in both visible and invisible ways. The sun's golden rays filtered through the haze, illuminating fallen wings and shattered weapons that lay scattered like memories of a time when hope flickered bright. Seraphiel knelt amid the debris, his heart heavy with the weight of choices made and paths taken. The scents of earth and ash wafted through the air, mingling with the metallic tang of blood spilled in defense of humanity. The battle had been won, but at what cost?

He recalled fallen companions reduced to mere whispers of their former selves, their once-radiant forms now marred by shadows. Some had been lost to darkness, their hearts consumed by the chaos they had once sought to escape. As he ran a hand over the ground, feeling the rough texture of shattered dreams and ambitions, he understood that the costs were beyond mere physical loss; they were etched into the fabric of their souls.

Nearby, Liora stood with her eyes closed, letting the soft breeze caress her face. The visions she had once received were now clouded, as if obscured by the same smoke that lingered in the air. Each revelation had guided her actions, pushing her toward a destiny that felt both monumental and overwhelming. The remnants of the battle stirred within her, unearthing doubts and fears that she thought she had buried. She had seen beings of immense power clash, witnessing sacrifices made in the name of a fragile peace. Now, standing alone amidst the chaos, she grappled with the aftermath of her own choices.

"Did we choose the right path?" she whispered, questioning the very nature of their conflict. The earlier exhilaration of battle faded, leaving only the jarring echo of loss in its wake. What was the worth of victory if it meant becoming something we swore to battle against?

Across the battlefield, Ezekiel examined the shadows of scarred trees, their twisted limbs resembling grasping hands yearning for release from the pain. Guardian angel though he was, he felt the burden of the world weighing down on him, chafing at the edges of his spirit. He had fought tirelessly, not just for humanity but for the brethren he had lost. The memories of bravery were quickly swallowed by the shadows of betrayal and heartache. In his heart, a tempest raged — a desire for redemption clashed with the realization of failure.

"I should have seen it coming," he muttered, kicking at a rock that lay in his path. Each step felt like a reminder of what could have been. If he had been more vigilant and acted sooner, might things have turned out differently? But now, these thoughts lingered like a specter, haunting him, a reflection of the choices made during the chaotic clash.

Seraphiel, still kneeling, sought to anchor himself amid the storm of his thoughts. He stared into the distance and saw Azazel emerging from the shadows. The fallen angel's once-majestic wings were now tattered and dark, yet his presence still commanded an unsettling gravity. Even in defeat, he retained an aura of cunning and wit, an embodiment of chaos wrapped in a veneer of misunderstood aspirations.

"Do you not feel it, Seraphiel?" Azazel's voice rang out, smooth yet laced with a sharp edge. "The exhilaration of breaking free? We are no longer bound by chains of righteousness. We exist now on the fringes, where power belongs to those bold enough to seize it."

Seraphiel met his gaze, irritation flaring within him. "Is this what the cost of freedom looks like, Azazel? Ruin? Destruction? The shadows mock us as we are buried beneath the weight of our choices."

With a smirk that faded into a grimace, Azazel continued, "Freedom is never without cost. You are so consumed by guilt that you fail to see the potential for rebirth. The heavens have denounced us, but the Earth welcomes those willing to adapt."

The world was changing, and with it, the reverberations of their choices would play out, challenging the very foundations of existence. Liora, still standing with her eyes closed, felt the pull of an impending storm, a sense of shifting tides. The world was coming alive with the energy of renewal, even amidst a background of chaos.

"Every choice we make builds a new path," she observed, her voice stronger than before. "We cannot forget the cost, but we must move forward, despite it."

Ezekiel looked at her, sensing the transformation igniting within her. "What do you suggest we do? This power we have—it can be both a blessing and a curse."

"In every wound lies a chance for healing," Liora declared, her heart steadying. "To rebuild and remember."

In that moment, she felt the weight of the prophecy align with her words. They had a choice: to absorb the lessons of the past and create a new legacy, or to succumb to despair and allow darkness to rewrite their narrative.

With a deeper sense of purpose blossoming in her chest, Liora turned to face the remnants of the battlefield. "First, we must address the scars, the wounds inflicted upon this realm and ourselves. Forgiveness must emerge from the ashes, or else we are doomed to repeat our failures."

Seraphiel nodded slowly, recognizing the truth in her statement. "But can we forgive ourselves, let alone those who fell and those we lost?"

As if in answer, a voice chimed in from the sidelines — a voice belonging to one of the survivors of the battle. A young woman, flushed with the remnants of fear and courage, stepped forward. "We can, and we must! No change comes without sacrifice. The spirits of those who fought live on within us. We owe it to them to ensure that their legacy is one of strength, of a shared journey between realms."

"I am one of those lost in this struggle," another voice added, an older man whose eyes twinkled with wisdom born from pain. "But I also see how this conflict has the potential to unite us. The scars may remain as marks of our trials, but if we acknowledge them, we can turn them into symbols of resilience."

Ezekiel observed the crowd of remnants beginning to gather. They were a mix of human and celestial, each one scarred but alive, each one carrying the burden of their choices heavily on their shoulders yet galvanizing within their hearts a nascent hope. The confrontation had altered them, but it had also ignited a fire that could bring about change.

In that moment, beneath a nascent sky painted with hopeful hues, Ezekiel felt a flicker of inspiration. "Together, we must forge a new understanding. We shall remember those we lost but not allow them to haunt us; instead, we honor them by building bridges across the realms."

Azazel shifted, intrigued by the unfolding unity. "And what will this alliance bring?"

"Perhaps," Liora interjected, "we can truly learn from each other. You say chaos leads to strength, but we have found strength in compassion and understanding. There is another way forward."

As they spoke, the air around them reverberated with possibilities. The presence of the fallen angel and guardian felt electric yet tenuous, a fragile tether that hinted at forging new alliances; disparate beings banding together in shared purpose.

"But how?" Seraphiel broke in, his voice laced with skepticism. "The wounds run too deep. The animosities are old. Can they truly be healed?"

With an unexpected clarity, Azazel frowned. "It starts with honesty. Of acknowledging our overlaps, our intersections, and distinguishing truth from deception."

"No more secrets," Liora stated. "If we are to find peace, we must lay bare our histories, our struggles, and our intentions. This will foster empathy, and together we can build a future that celebrates both realms."

A quiet buzz of agreement washed over the group as ideas began to flow, filled with the promise of reconciliation. Each being took a deep breath, acknowledging their histories yet setting their sights on the greater horizon. The journey to repair what had been broken was daunting, but it was a journey they could undertake together.

With every voice that stepped forward and every story that was shared, that sense of shared vulnerability laid the groundwork for a bond forged in understanding, teeth gritted with determination as they navigated their complex legacies. The pain wasn't forgotten, but it was acknowledged; it became part of their shared narrative.

In the following weeks, they worked tirelessly to remedy the destruction wrought by the battle. Angels and humans collaborated to restore the land, planting seeds of both crops and hope. They drew upon their unique strengths: while angels healed, guiding healing energies through the land, humans labored alongside them, imbuing the soil with resilience.

And in the evenings, as the sun dipped below the horizon, they would gather around fires, sharing tales of heroism and loss, reliving their stories — a testament to the power of memory and the necessity of community.

Through these shared rituals—of rebuilding and renewal—the shadows faded gradually. For with each act of solidarity, something sacred emerged from the ashes; the ties that bound them grew stronger.

Yet, beneath the surface, echoes of the past still lingered, and forgiveness was not always easily granted. Tension sometimes flickered at the edge of conversations when history reared its head, igniting old grievances. Azazel often found himself at the center of ire, both from angels who could not forget his actions and from humans suspicious of his motives.

In these moments, Seraphiel would step forward, his voice steadied by newfound understanding. "The balance between light and shadow dwells within each of us. Our paths are never as simple as they once seemed. Let not our fears define us."

As they rebuilt, weary hearts began to open, sharing their vulnerabilities and acknowledging their hidden scars. Forgiveness, too, emerged quietly, taking root in the fertile soil of empathy. Peace, they realized, was not an endpoint, but a journey, undertaken with intention and grace.

And as seasons changed, so too did the landscapes of their souls. They found laughter again amidst the ashes, renewed connections born out of once-sundered pasts. Bonds of friendship and allegiance were forged, painting a tapestry of unity that defied the boundaries of light and shadow. They became more than enemies seeking reconciliation—they became co-creators of a destiny shaped by understanding.

The world they inhabited was forever changed, but while the scars remained, the vibrant hues of resilience triumphed. Little by little, through the overarching weight of loss, they grew into something profound, discovering strength in their shared humanity and divine intricacies.

And so, the realms began to hum a new tune, echoing with whispers of connection that beckoned forth a brighter tomorrow—a whisper that held the promise of reconciliation, not as the resolve of one battle fought, but as the promise of ongoing transformation in a universe still coming to terms with its own complexities.

Together, they dared to dream anew, igniting the spark that would light the path toward healing. As the dawn of possibilities glimmered ever so slightly on the horizon, it beckoned them—the very essence of their journey—with the knowledge that while old scars may remain, new beginnings could bloom, just waiting for a chance to rise.

A New Dawn

As dawn broke over the remnants of a once-chaotic battlefield, the air shimmered with an ethereal light—a stark contrast to the devastation that had marked the night before. Ashes drifted like fallen petals, and the distant echoes of the conflict faded, replaced by a silence heavy with promise. This was not merely a new day; it was a new dawn—a herald of change that swept across the realms, intertwining fates and forging unlikely alliances.

Seraphiel hovered above the scarred landscape, his once-luminous wings now a muted shade of silver, still touched by the shadows of chaos but glimmering with the potential of redemption. He surveyed the scene below—fallen allies and enemies alike were strewn across the ground, bodies marked not only by battle but by the emotional scars of choices made under duress. As dawn's warmth enveloped him, he felt a stirring within, a call to action unlike any he had experienced before.

His thoughts turned to Liora, the young woman who had become a beacon of light amidst darkness. She had stood at the forefront of the battle, wielding her visions not as weapons but as guides. They had first met when her visions were unclear, mere echoes of the looming conflict. Now, as he focused on the horizon, he could see her rising from the ashes of that battle alongside her fellow humans, embodying the hope that this new dawn promised.

Liora stood amongst the rubble, watching as the first rays of sunlight illuminated her surroundings. The memories of those she had lost weighed heavily on her heart, but she also felt a sense of purpose awakening within her. The conflict that had raged through the realms had revealed the power of unity; it had unveiled the strength born from the ashes of despair. Around her, people gathered—once-terrified citizens transformed into warriors, their courage ignited by the idea of standing for something greater than themselves.

"Can you believe it?" A voice broke through her thoughts. It was Nathan, an old friend who had once doubted her visions. "We actually did it. We're alive!"

"Yes," Liora replied, a smile breaking through her somber demeanor. "But there is much still to be done. We must ensure this peace holds. We can't allow ourselves to be divided ever again."

As if echoing her resolve, the figures of Seraphiel and Azazel emerged from the shadows, the former glowing faintly with remnants of celestial light, the latter enveloped in a palpable darkness that seemed to ebb and flow like the tide. Azazel's expression, once filled with malice, had softened, revealing the weight of introspection that now marked his features. Today, he was not the contradiction of chaos that everyone had come to fear; he was a creature transformed, a being seeking understanding.

"We must talk," Seraphiel said, his voice tinged with authority, yet warmer than in times past. It was this warmth that drew the attention of Liora and the surrounding humans, who regarded Azazel with both curiosity and trepidation. He knew the challenges that lay ahead; they had only just begun to mend the rift between realms.

Azazel stepped forward, his gaze layered with remorse. "I've seen enough fire and ruin to last several lifetimes. We're not just shadows battling light anymore; we need to redefine what it means to exist alongside one another."

With Seraphiel's encouragement, Liora stepped into the center of the gathering. "It's time for us to listen," she announced, her voice carrying authority born from conviction. "We've learned that there's a delicate balance between light and dark, between hope and despair. Each of us has a role to play in reshaping our destinies, but we can only do so together."

Tension hung in the air, but it was different now—a tension framed by anticipation rather than fear. The humans exchanged glances, finding courage in their shared experience and the transformation they were witnessing in Azazel.

"I know I've caused pain," Azazel began, his voice steady but filled with emotion. "I was once consumed by ambition and power, blinded to the suffering I inflicted. But I've realized that even the darkest hearts can seek redemption. If you're willing to accept it, I'll follow Seraphiel's lead. I want to help heal the rift that I played a part in widening."

Seraphiel placed a hand on Azazel's shoulder, anchoring him in this moment of vulnerability. "Forgiveness is a powerful force, and so is the willingness to change. We all share responsibility for our pasts, but what matters now is the future. We must instill in each other the virtues of understanding and compassion."

The sun rose higher, its rays cascading across the battlefield, illuminating the faces of both angels and humans. Liora felt a spark of hope swelling within her—this was their chance to build something remarkable from the ashes.

"Let us hold a council," Liora suggested, her voice ringing strong. "We need to gather representatives from every faction—the humans, the angels, and even those who have walked the darker paths. We must voice our fears and hopes, and create agreements that will protect our realms."

The assemblage broke into varied murmurs, uncertainty lingering in the air. Yet, Seraphiel stepped beside her, raising his voice over the crowd. "Liora speaks the truth. We must bridge the divides; only then can we forge alliances where unity can thrive. We need to create a charter of peace—a pledge that we will always strive for understanding over conflict."

It was a radical proposition, but as the first rays of hope washed over them, the crowd responded with nods and murmurs of agreement. Liora felt a thrill of excitement; this moment could redefine their shared destiny.

As the council took shape, representatives from all walks of life stepped forward—some hesitant, others emboldened by the role they had to play in this new world. There were brave warriors, former demons seeking redemption, and even scholars from distant lands ready to lend their wisdom. Each voice added to the tapestry of their intentions, painting a clearer picture of how they could work toward a future of unity.

"A charter of peace," said Nathan, his voice steady as he stood beside Liora. "But let's not merely focus on words; we must implement measures that will hold us accountable. Our past missteps should embolden us to move forward together, laying down a framework of coexistence."

"And what if darkness seeks to disrupt our peace?" one of the former warriors interjected, their gaze locked onto Azazel. "How can we trust those who once aligned with such chaos?"

"Trust begins with understanding," Azazel responded, his tone firm yet earnest. "Let me show you that I can stand with you against any threats. My past is not my only identity. I will work to protect this peace and ensure that our children do not experience the horror of conflict."

Time stretched into moments of passionate debate, voices rising and falling in a symphony of hope and skepticism. With each passing hour, a picture of their future began to take form—a tapestry woven not in isolation, but in connection, fraught with imperfection yet steadfast in intention.

As the day unfolded, the sun painted the sky in shades of gold, signaling an unyielding sense of hope. Liora stood at the front, her heart swelling with emotion as she witnessed the forging of the new council—people once divided now finding common ground through shared experiences of pain, loss, and ultimately, love for their realms.

With a deep breath, Liora opened herself to the unseen currents that had guided her throughout this journey. Glancing toward Seraphiel, she recognized the mirror of change in his eyes. "This isn't just about preventing conflict; it's about nurturing understanding. How can we instill compassion in the hearts of generations to come?"

Seraphiel met her gaze, the weight of his choices visible in the depths of his eyes. "We start with education and engagement. We create a society where stories of our past inform the present. We will craft a new mythology together—one that emphasizes unity rather than separation."

The call for the council's establishment echoed through the morning light, resonating within each heart present. The celestial and earthly beings alike felt a collective shift within them, rekindling hope for a future rewritten.

Weeks passed as the treaty of reconciliation took shape, and while tensions remained, the council worked tirelessly. They organized gatherings to promote understanding, where angels shared the mysteries of their realms and narrators recounted the tales of monsters who had been given a chance at redemption.

Seraphiel and Azazel often stood side by side, presenting their intertwined stories to the assembly. They met skepticism and hope, fear and curiosity, and through their courage to be vulnerable, they began to build a bridge, spanning the gap that had once divided them.

Liora, acting as a catalyst for healing, immersed herself in community work, helping to forge friendships among the previously fractured groups. At the center of her efforts was a school—a place where humans and angels could learn from one another, where young minds would be taught the value of coexistence.

One evening, under a starlit sky, Liora gathered her students in the garden of the newly established inter-realm academy. The air buzzed with laughter and curiosity as children from both realms chased one another, their shouts mingling freely, unencumbered by the weight of prior grudges.

She looked up, taking in the sight of her students nourished by the teachings of cooperation. It filled her with profound joy, knowing she was nurturing a generation that would grow without the shadow of hatred looming over them.

Seraphiel joined her, observing the mingling of wings and laughter, light and shadow. "We have much to be grateful for," he murmured, pride illuminating his features. "The seeds we plant today will take root in the generations to come."

"But what of those who still harbor darkness in their hearts?" Liora asked, leaning against the garden's ancient oak tree. "How do we confront them without fear?"

"As we have learned through conflict, the greatest battles often take place within ourselves," he replied softly. "We must remember that change is a journey. We can guide others toward the light through compassion, even when their paths seem shrouded in darkness."

Liora felt a wave of conviction surge through her. "And we must keep telling our stories—the stories of redemption and the power of unity. Only then can we remind others that we're all part of the same tapestry."

As the stars twinkled above them, Seraphiel reached out, resting his hand gently on her shoulder. "And so it begins. Each dawn brings new possibilities and the chance for harmony—if we are willing to embrace it."

Months flowed into years, and the realms began to heal, marred only by the occasional reminders of pain but bolstered by the resolve to foster understanding. The council became a foundation of hope, growing in number and influence as it expanded beyond the borders of their respective realms.

Together, they organized global events to celebrate the amalgamation of cultures—festivals where humans danced under celestial lights, and angels painted the night sky with breathtaking displays of harmony. Yet, more importantly, they instilled in their children the significance of bridging divides that had once seemed insurmountable.

Then, one fateful evening, a figure appeared at the gates of their gathering— a shadow lurking amid the light. It was a creature reminiscent of Azazel in some ways, but more grotesque, more chaotic—the embodiment of all their past fears that had been cast aside. Whispers of treachery washed over the crowd, echoing remnants of what had once been.

But as Seraphiel, Liora, and Azazel stepped forward hand in hand, something shifted. The whispers softened, and the embodiment of darkness faltered. Power, once forged from fear and division, found its strength dissipating in the warmth of connection.

Deep within, an understanding blossomed—a realization that even the most overbearing shadows could lose their grip if faced with unyielding light. And so, just as a new dawn had emerged years before, another awaited them on the horizon.

The embodiment of darkness turned its gaze from them to the rising sun; its form shifted, wavering as if haunted by the specter of hope. Through connection and the lessons learned in unity, even those steeped in shadows could begin their journey toward the light.

As dawn unfurled above them, bathed in ethereal hues of pink and gold, Liora felt certainty swell within her heart. They had embarked on a journey without end—a continuous renewal of hope, a promise that even the deepest divides could be bridged, that no one was destined to remain lost in darkness.

This was their new dawn—the blossoming of a world reborn, woven together by the threads of understanding, compassion, and the enduring pursuit of peace. The battle between good and evil would endure, but each dawn would bring with it the potential for reconciliation instead of ruin, inviting all beings to contribute to a story still waiting to be written.

— — —

Thank You for Joining the Adventure

You made it to the other side of the veil.

In a world that pulls your attention in every direction, you gave hours of yours to this story. That is not something I take lightly, and I appreciate you.

My hope is that something in these pages stayed with you. A question you did not have before. A character whose weight felt familiar. A moment where the line between myth and something older, something real, felt thinner than you expected.

The story you just read came from much searching. From sitting with ancient texts, hard questions, and letting scripture speak without the filter of tradition. What was revealed did not come all at once. It came in layers, each one opening something deeper than the last.

That search is not finished. Neither is what it produces. There is more being revealed.

I am grateful you were here for this part of the journey.

With gratitude,

Shawn

About the Author

Shawn Kelly is a Designer in the offshore energy industry.

He grew up Catholic, always believing, but never quite fitting in. Through every season of wandering there was an ever praying mother asking Yahuah to guide her son's path.

He is a man who thinks deeply, studies ancient texts, and asks questions most people walk past without stopping. The Torah. The Book of Enoch. The Dead Sea Scrolls. The layers of scripture sitting just outside what most people were never taught. When he found them, they did not feel new. They felt like the rest of a sentence he had been reading his whole life.

Angels and Monsters is a story that came from that.

He calls Houston, Texas home with his children Daniel, Abigail, and Jacob.

You can connect with me on:

🌐 https://nexushousemedia.com

 https://www.facebook.com/LKELLYHARLEY

🔗 https://www.instagram.com/angels.and.monsters.bookseries

Subscribe to my newsletter:

✉ https://nexushousemedia.com/contact